LOVE ON THE SWEEPING PLAINS

A NOVELLA FROM LOVE IN THE SUNBURNT LAND ANTHOLOGY

LEANNE LOVEGROVE

SMALL TOWN PUBLISHING

LOVE ON THE SWEEPING PLAINS

LEANNE LOVEGROVE

1

———

ori Christensen banged on the glass sliding door. It rattled under the pressure, but no one came.

The dazzling morning sun beat down upon her back and moisture gathered in the dip between her breasts. Her reflection glared back at her and she knocked again, pausing before shading her eyes and squinting to see through the pane.

'Hello!' she shouted.

Nothing. Not a shadow, nor a murmur from inside. Glancing around, she registered the sign above the door that read *Cedar Creek Plains Vet Surgery* in faded red ink. Surely they were open.

She glanced at her wristwatch. Shit. Maybe not. It seemed later but it wasn't yet eight o'clock. They'd been driving for hours.

The two tiny animals she cupped in her other hand didn't make a sound. She shook them, hoping for a miracle. When had they stopped squeaking? Hiccupped sobs rose from the little girl beside her who gripped her skirt.

Tori thumped on the glass harder until the crunch of boots

on loose gravel behind her caused her to swirl around, her heart hammering hard in her chest.

A tall, lanky man carrying a bulky camera on his shoulder raced towards her across the carpark, fumbling over his undone shoelaces. If he didn't fall over his own feet, the size of the camera would topple him at any moment.

Tori released a breath. It wasn't Todd. Of course it wasn't. Thank goodness. She was being ridiculous peering over her shoulder like a nervous ninny.

But who was this guy carrying a movie camera? And where was his pet?

As he reached her the man manoeuvred the camera off his shoulder, fiddling with a couple of buttons before positioning the equipment back in place. He loomed the lens so close to her face she veered backwards.

'Who are you?' And, just in case, she asked, 'Did Todd send you?'

Mirabelle howled louder and tugged on her skirt.

Out of the corner of her eye she caught a shadow move inside so Tori knocked again, rapping until her knuckles hurt.

The glass panel slid open. *Phew*. She jostled on her feet, ready to race inside but the figure stepped forward into the daylight and she stopped.

Zac.

It took a moment for her brain to catch up. Zachary Coleman. Her mouth opened and shut, her eyes blinking a few times too many.

He was still here. The quintessential country boy and lad next door. Her first kiss.

Embarrassment and shame washed over her as if it was yesterday. Heat crawled up her neck and she flushed.

Of course, Zac was the town vet. That was all he'd ever wanted.

And now he here was in front of her. And she needed a vet.

How strange she'd ended up here first. She'd never contemplated making a mad dash to the surgery before arriving in town. Damn pets. How was she to know they might croak it on the trip?

Neither had she thought coming home would erase all memories of the past, had she? No, but she hadn't expected them to be thrown up in her face so fast. *Welcome home, Tori.*

'Victoria?' He'd always called her by her full name. Always so polite. And she loved the way it rolled off his tongue.

Zac's brow creased in confusion.

He hadn't changed. Same blonde tousled locks that he wore too long and maybe a few more lines around his eyes and across his forehead. But he still resembled the boy she remembered. Focusing on his face, she saw his lips move. Those lips transported her back in time and she remembered the feel of them against hers and how much she'd enjoyed it.

Oh God, a thrill raced straight through her.

'Is this the first contestant? I was told they weren't arriving until this afternoon...' came a muffled voice from behind the lens.

'What?' Zac turned his attention to behind her and lifted one hand to place in front of the camera, preventing it capturing the unfolding scene. 'No,' he said.

Undeterred, the cameraman shifted position to avoid Zac's hand and kept shooting.

'What are you doing here?' Zac asked her.

A good question. It brought her back to earth.

The guinea pigs!

'Can you save them?' Tori held up the duo of what she hoped were not lifeless furry bodies.

'Oh, you have a sick animal. Of course, come on in.'

Why else would she rock up to the vet surgery at this hour?

Zac ushered them inside towards a consulting room. Mirabelle was sniffling but trailed behind, followed by the camera guy.

Zac slammed the clinic door shut and blocked him out. 'Man, that's not the deal…' the cameraman yelled.

He took the two creatures from Tori. They were tiny in his large hands and he placed them on the examination table with care. Mirabelle moved in closer beside him and peered up with those large round almond eyes of hers. Wet trails made their way down her dirty cheeks and she stifled a further sob before rising on her tiptoes. She was so small she couldn't see over the table. Zac paused, watched her and then dragged over a chair and lifted her up.

'Are these your pets?'

The little girl in her fairy outfit nodded. 'Are they sick?'

'I don't know. Let's have a look.'

The door opened a tiny crack and the camera lens snuck in; the man's legs visible underneath.

'Get out!' Zac yelled and Tori jumped.

'Who is that guy?' she asked.

Bent over, he glanced up through his long floppy fringe. The gaze that seared into her asked a thousand questions. Tori balanced from foot to foot, uncomfortable with his scrutiny.

'It's a long story,' he answered and went back to work.

'I think,' and this time he addressed Mirabelle, 'these guys went a little too long without water. So, I'm going to give them a big drink.'

'Oh, thank goodness. They're going to be okay, aren't they, Zac?'

Mirabelle inched closer and leaned her elbows on the table to watch his every move. Tori did too and propped herself against the hard bench.

Once the guinea pigs were hooked up to some fluid, he said, 'I think they'll be okay. They'll need to stay here for a few hours for observation. Are you in town long?' This question was for her. He rose up tall and waited.

'Um, yes, maybe. I'm staying at Nanna's, of course. I'm so grateful. Thank you, Zac. We'd all be very unhappy if these little critters hadn't made the journey with us.' She stroked the curly, dark hair of her daughter as she spoke, avoiding Zac's eye. 'When should I come back and collect them?'

Tori tried to focus on the detail of what Zac was saying. Instead, she became intensely aware of every detail around them. Where Zac put his hands. His Adam's apple as it bobbed when he spoke. How he scratched the itch on his back. The clean medical smell of the surgery. It's too bright whiteness. The sterile instruments lined up on the side table in the room and the timbre of his voice. And suddenly the room was suffocating her. This town had that effect. She hadn't been back for five minutes and already it was getting to her. Already she was morphing back into the young woman she once was. The young innocent girl that had once lived in this town.

And fled.

Zac chatted to Mirabelle allowing Tori to get lost in her daydream. Every now and then he furtively glanced up as if checking she was still there. Fair enough, she deserved that. In the middle of a sentence, Mirabelle turned to her. 'Mummy, can we take Puddles?'

'Mummy?' the words slid off his tongue. She jerked her head up and held her chin too high. Defensive perhaps?

Yes. Circumstances had changed and so had she.

'Yep. This little rascal is Mirabelle, my daughter,' and she clasped the girl's hand.

Time for them to go. She needed to let her erratic heart calm the hell down and pull herself together. She tugged her daughter towards the door. 'We can't thank you enough…'

Zac strode ahead and reached for the door handle. For a crazy moment she thought he was preventing their exit. Did he want her to stay? Ridiculous. He turned the knob and moved aside to let them go first.

The doorframe wasn't large and Tori's hips brushed against his hand. A rush of warmth spread to her erogenous zones. She glanced up, fearing he could tell. Zac continued to watch her. Did he hold his breath?

Before the door had fully opened, the guy jumped up from the plastic waiting-room chair, camera in position, the red light on top flashing.

Her eyes on him, Zac shrugged. 'It's a reality TV show.'

2

———————

Tori parked her car off to the side of the long drive to her nan's B & B. She let the dust settle and focused ahead, on the house. Tears pricked her eyes and a funny excited flutter went crazy in her tummy.

She hadn't been home for years. So many, she'd lost count. Long before Mirabelle, four years old, had been born anyway.

The place appeared the same; worn, but welcoming. Her nan's house was rusty red and it contrasted against a vibrant blue sky and sat on a pillow of verdant grass. Occasionally there was a spot of white as a duck or a lamb or a goat wandered past.

On the outskirts of *Cedar Creek Plains*, the farmhouse stood solitary, an upright double-storey timber building lumped in the middle of broad, golden sweeping plains. The plains that had named the town surrounded the area on all sides.

The smell of bacon wafted out through the open kitchen windows, the aromas mixing in with smoke billowing from the chimney. Her stomach turned. She sure was back on the farm and undeniably in the country. Trying to distract her senses from the frying pork, she listened to the chickens clucking and laying their morning eggs. The familiar sounds of a new day.

'Out,' Mirabelle sang from the back seat.

She was *home*. Her nan's home anyway. Where she was raised.

Tori reached in and extracted Mirabelle from her car seat and bunched her up in her arms for a quick cuddle. She checked her daughter's face. She seemed to be coping okay, but who knew. It hadn't been very long and her father was unlikely to be a distant memory yet.

'Let's go and find Nan.' Mirabelle nodded, giggling as a noisy duck crossed their path, its loud quacks resounding across the yard.

Entering through the back door, the cooking smell became overwhelming and Tori gagged.

Her nan was bent over the old-style aga cooker.

'Nan!' she called out when Rosalie didn't hear them enter.

Her nan turned and a broad smile opened up her face. Dropping the spatula onto the bench, she rushed towards them.

'Tori. Mirabelle. What a lovely surprise!' She squeezed Tori into a tight hug, the type only a loving grandmother can offer, before bending low to Mirabelle and kissing her sweet cheeks.

The skillet hissed and exploded.

'Oh, bugger. You'll never believe it. Helena, the girl who helps me out around here, usually cooks and tidies up, hasn't turned up this morning. I've got a few guests in and more arriving today to a full house.' Rosalie Stanhope fluttered her arms like a bird and turned back to the stove.

'I can help,' Tori offered and retrieved an apron off the back of the door and searched the pantry for ingredients. 'You finish off the bacon though, and I'll prepare something else. Remind me what you usually serve for breakfast?'

Nan giggled. 'Are you still on that silly diet?'

'Nan, it's not a diet. I'm vegan. I don't belong to a cult. A lot of people don't eat meat or dairy these days.'

With her back turned, Nan said, 'Maybe in the city, but not the country. We haven't advanced that far yet. A wee bit set in our ways. I'm sure your poor pet would love a rasher of bacon, nice and crispy on a slice of buttered white bread. You used to love it as a child.'

'I loved a lot of things as a kid. Didn't mean they were good for me.'

Already she was whisking and mixing. Calm washed over her and happiness at being in the kitchen; anyone's kitchen, although her nan's was pretty special.

'Well, the bacon is done anyhow. How about I take little Mirry out to feed the animals and collect the fresh eggs and you can finish up in here?'

Mirabelle squealed with delight and placed her tiny hand in Nan's. She'd loved doing the same when she was small. *Back then, before.* She smiled watching them leave, then opened all the windows to rid the kitchen of the odour of over-cooked pork.

'Nan, is it okay if we stay for a while?'

The breakfast rush was over, relaxing, they sat together on the spacious front deck, enjoying a cuppa. Green tea for Tori.

'Will Todd join you?'

'No.'

Nan waited, maintaining the silence. She was good at that.

'You'll never believe what happened.' Tori looked away to hold in the tears that threatened. 'I busted him having sex with the new Pilates instructor in the change rooms at work. I can't get the image out of my mind. All bronzed skin and platinum blonde hair and pert breasts! How could he do that to me, Nan? To Mirry?'

'Ouch. The bastard. Can't say I'm surprised though. He was a nice bloke but a bit light on. Maybe too nice, hey, to all of the girls. What will you do now?'

'Dunno. I'm not sure yet. But I intend to get myself sorted with some good old-fashioned country living for the time being. And maybe lots of Nanna cuddles.'

Nan turned serious and placed her palm over hers. 'Oh, Tori. It's wonderful to have you back. I miss you and you're always welcome here. It'll be nice to bring some life back into the old place with some young blood.'

'Yeah, and don't worry about finding someone else to help out. I'll do it. That's how I'll earn my keep. Obviously I'm skint and have no job, but you won't turf me out for not contributing will you?'

It was supposed to be a joke. She thought her nan got it.

'I'll eat your organic vegetable food if it means you're cooking,' Nan offered a cheeky smile and continued, 'that sounds perfect, love, thank you.'

Tori searched the yard for Mirry who wasn't used to all the space. The country was nothing like the congested and built-up city. So much room to breathe.

Mirabelle swung on the old rubber tyre hanging from the oak in the front yard. Her long hair flew behind her with each swing and she giggled with glee.

'That could be you out there. She is so like you as a child.'

'We had a bit of an incident on the way out. Mirabelle has two pet guinea pigs. I put them in a box with her in the back-seat. Who knew they couldn't survive a few hours without food and drink? Most animals can, can't they? Anyway, as we entered town they were lifeless and not moving. I stopped at the vet surgery. Zac is the town vet.' She stated it as a question.

'Yes.'

'You never told me.'

'You haven't been concerned with the news around here since you left. I tried a few times to keep you informed but you weren't interested.'

'That's not true. I was probably distracted with other issues.' But Tori knew that wasn't the case. After leaving, she didn't want to associate herself with the old hick town she'd grown up in. She'd fled to a new, better life. Or so she thought.

Nan didn't respond. A goat approached Mirabelle and she crouched and tried to pat its fur but pulled her hand away each time it moved closer. They all had some adjusting to do.

'Well, okay. Whatever. I'm knocking on the door not realising it wasn't open yet and the strangest thing happened. A cameraman appeared from the carpark and flashed his camera in my face. Zac seemed annoyed but said it had to do with some reality TV show.'

'Oh yes!' Nan slapped her knee. 'That's what's happening today. They're my guests. It's a scoop. The four young girls are staying here for the duration of the show.' She chuckled. 'Imagine,' and she swept her arms wide, '*Cedar Creek Plains Farm Stay and B & B* is the next bachelorette pad. It might make me famous. Be good for future bookings at least. Well, if we can pull it off.' She sat up and placed her tea on the low set outdoor table. 'What a time for Helena to go missing.'

'What on earth are you talking about? Why is the farm going to be a bachelorette pad for a vet doco?'

Nan sat back then. 'It's not a vet doco. It's like one of those reality dating shows. But a country one.' She clasped her hands together trying to remember the name and muttering under her breath.

A light sheen of perspiration broke out across Tori's brow. The sun was high in the sky now, bearing down upon them from its orange orb. The heat of the country was like no other. Another wash of nostalgia came over her of long hot summer days, running around barefoot playing games until diving into the river to cool off.

'*Local Lads Looking for Love*! That's it. It's a regional show, not a fancy one like *Bachelor* or *Farmer Wants a Wife*. This one is local lads.'

'You're telling me Zachary Coleman is a contestant on a local dating show and his prospective girlfriends are staying here. For how long?' Tori detected the high intonation in her voice.

'A month!'

Tori took a large gulp of her tea that burned her throat on the way down.

'The cabins are ready but need a last check. I have some lovely flowers fresh from the garden to be placed in vases. Nothing like a homely touch.' Her nan stood and got moving. There was no stopping the old girl. You'd easily forget she was well into her seventies.

3

'So, looking for love, huh, doc? Today might be your lucky day!' Bert the servo attendant sang out as Zac filled the ute. It was the third gibe this morning already. He held his hand up acknowledging the joke. The old fellow guffawed.

To top it off that bloody annoying cameraman tailed him and moved with surprising agility between Bert and the bowser. Did people really want to watch him pumping fuel?

After cornering the guy this morning, Zac had settled down. The poor man was doing his job. And his job was apparently to follow his every move. Get footage of a day in the usual life of Zac Coleman, *Cedar Creek Plains* vet and local, and contestant on the inaugural *Local Lads Looking for Love* show.

He had two thoughts about this – first, he wanted to kill his interfering younger sisters and secondly, it was likely to be a boring and short show if they wanted exciting footage of his life.

Zac fought the urge to jump in the car and race away to lose the cameraman. But that wasn't fair to the poor bloke, and at the end of the day, he'd agreed to this crazy scheme.

Best he forget about it and get on with his day.

He turned his mind back to his home visit. Unfortunately, it was to the Coleman cattle Station. His mum had rung, not his dad, and asked him to do his regular check-ups. He hadn't stayed home last night instead sleeping at the vet clinic. What a blessing! The head vet, Rob Cooper, otherwise known as Chief, was away and he'd bunked in his quarters. And he'd stay there until the boss returned from his fancy cruise.

Zac wasn't sure he could deal with his father today. It had been a strange morning already.

Victoria.

He'd waited years for her to return and she never had. Now she was here. The same day he was about to embark on a ridiculous love show. A show he was reluctant to be involved in. Oh, the irony.

With one hand on the steering wheel, Zac fiddled with the ring on his pinkie finger and pictured the older, more mature Victoria. She'd aged; he had too. Was it possible she'd become more beautiful? And she was a mother. He'd heard the odd comment here or there over the years. But to be honest, he'd avoided the gossip. It had never served him well.

Zac wound down the window and let the cool air of the morning rush in. He travelled past the bakery, the pub, the bank and drove over the river that separated the town. In *Cedar Creek Plains* you either lived north or south of the river. His family property was north. The vet clinic south; Victoria's home south. It went without saying he preferred the southside of town.

The long, majestic driveway of Coleman Cattle Station approached and the fat, round bottle trees lining the drive came into view. More like the entrance to a royal palace. The station had always been out of place and overdone.

A few Angus cows sheltered under the trees and Zac pulled

up sharp, retrieved his phone from the glovebox and hopped out. With the sun filtering through the branches of the trees and the positioning of the cows, it was a perfect shot. He snapped, discarding a few dodgy images and sat in the driver's seat whilst he uploaded the pic.

#serenity #idylic #farmlife #cows

His brief stop caught the cameraman off guard and by the time Zac posted the shot, the man was still fumbling around with his camera from the boot. Zac chuckled and drove off, leaving him by the side of the road.

He parked the ute in the circular drive and before he'd even had the chance to exit, Holly and Lara bolted out the door.

'Why are you working today? You should be at home getting ready, showering and dressing for the big night!' Holly squealed into his ear and tugged on his arm.

Conscious of the footage being captured on camera, Zac acted all cool and stand offish. How much to give away?

He kissed Holly on the cheek but didn't reply. Did likewise to Lara. 'Can't wait to hear how it goes,' she yelled as she departed for the primary school where she worked as a teacher. She blew him a cheeky kiss.

'Should I come over later and help you choose your clothes?' Holly asked.

'No.'

'Aw, come on, it will be fun.'

'No way. I think you've done enough little sister.'

His father walked around from the sheds and the banter stopped. Holly took off and he extracted his gear from the car.

This time he waited for the camera. This footage he could deal with – him doing what he did best.

Tori knew she shouldn't, but it was like the show was playing out in front of her.

One of the girls, no, *woman*, looked towards the farmhouse and Tori dropped the curtain to avoid detection. It was stifling in the kitchen as she prepped for the welcome dinner and she pulled her long hair back into a makeshift pony, holding it away from her neck. The relief was immediate but she was pretending to be distracted and glanced out the window again. She did live here after all, but to be found snooping, no that wasn't cool. And why was she peeking anyway? Curiosity was the answer.

The group of four women exited the shiny black Prado and circled around themselves, taking in their home for the next month. Tori tried to imagine what they saw. She guessed it depended on where they came from. For a country girl there'd be no surprises but what about a city girl. A culture shock?

She admired the four eligible women and wondered what type Zac preferred. She didn't know. When she'd left town all those years ago, he'd been dating her best friend, Susie. Susie had been the quintessential country gal, all long legs and leather-brown skin and hair bleached from the outdoors. Country life was in her blood from centuries ago.

Whereas she'd always been the odd one out. Dark hair, dark eyes, exotic French influence from the father she never knew while her mother was fair like her nan. And the glasses she couldn't see without making her a geek. Not the fun-loving kid who ran carefree through the fields. Tori was the one to fall over, scrape her knee and end up worse for wear. She'd given most things a good go, though. Maybe she was half tomboy.

At the time, Zac and Susie had seemed like a perfect match. Similar interests – both loved sport, commitment to their families with country living in their veins, a bright bold future ahead of them. What happened to Susie? To Tori's shame she hadn't kept in touch. It was all too hard when you were taking different paths. She was forging a life in the big city. A different life. Not to mention the guilt at what she'd done.

There had been one passionate, well, very passionate kiss between her and Zac on their graduation night. It had caught her by surprise but man, what a kiss. She still remembered every detail after all these years. Once their lips had touched, it was as if they'd let go a long-held passion for each other. Passion she certainly hadn't been aware of until he'd awakened her desire.

The kiss may have started fast and furious and a bit fumbly, like a roll in the hay, but it had ended tender, deep and oh so intimate. Tori swore she'd never been kissed like that since.

She held her left fingers up to her lips reliving the sensation and dropped them just as quickly.

Any recollection of that night and she hated herself. Cheating on your best friend and enjoying it – it doesn't get much worse. She blamed herself but how had Zac allowed it to happen when he'd been dating Susie? And now she knew what it was like to be cheated on. She was no better than her unfaithful husband. Back then, her penance had been to flee, escape the scene of the crime.

But that was a long time ago.

Today, she was married, had a child and was recently separated from her lying, cheating, filthy husband. The husband she'd loved; the husband who had introduced her to a new life; the man she credited with helping her find herself. But had she? Or had it all been convenient at the time?

How did these women compare?

One looked comfortable in her surrounds wearing jodhpurs and R.M William boots and an Akubra hat. Had to be a true-blue country chick. Based on appearances she might be a winner. The thought make Tori's chest go tight.

A blonde-haired girl giggled in a cute and feminine manner and the sound drifted in. Would Zac find her titter attractive? The woman was overdressed in a short skirt, small heels and too many bangles that jingled up her arm. Tori was sure she was a very nice girl.

Another wore her longish red hair in a loose bun with runners and her active gear appearing ready for a yoga workout.

The fourth lady was different to the rest and stood out. Goosepimples spread across Tori's arms. Would Zac appreciate her uniqueness? The woman had dark features but it was the way she held herself that caught Tori's attention. Tall, straight, elegant. Yes, beautiful.

Her nan entered the kitchen.

'Love, will you come and help me show the ladies to their cabins and explain the basics?'

'Sure. Are there cameras out there?'

'No. They've arrived alone with the host. She's a local TV journalist. Nice lady. I think the idea is to commence filming tonight at the welcome dinner. It's a big deal. You feeling okay about preparations?'

Oh yes, she was sure the ladies would love her vegan Bombay burritos and vegetable biryani.

4

———

Her mobile buzzed again. Tori pulled it out of her apron pocket and checked the screen. Todd, for the hundredth time. He'd been ringing all afternoon and she'd ignored him. She understood avoidance wasn't an option, and she'd accept his call when it suited her.

Now didn't suit.

And, what would she possibly say to him? Act all civil as if their relationship was hunky dory? Or God forbid – forgive him? Maybe she needed to wait and see what he said first. See if he apologised, begged her forgiveness and asked her to return? The whole thing gave her a headache and she needed to concentrate.

Tori whipped off the apron and flung the phone on the bench.

Not for a moment had she considered she'd be on TV. Pretty stupid when you remembered the television show's welcome dinner was at the farm. And this wasn't a fancy five-star restaurant with wait-staff. Her and Nan were the cooks and waiters and on clean-up duty. But as Nan reminded her numerous times that afternoon, they were being paid.

Murmurs of conversation drifted in from outside. The women had arrived at the homestead and were having a drink on the deck. The sun was slowly kissing the horizon and providing them with a golden glow. Tori had to admit it was a special scene. In every direction were sweeping plains of gold and green grass that billowed gently in the breeze. Bottlebrush trees grew sporadically breaking up the flat prairies. Their branches forming perfectly rounded foliage that was lush and heavy and coloured deeper than the grass it sat upon. The trees were framed by a sky of muted pink. Further in the distance the main street of town was evident, like an oasis in a desert.

Nan had jazz background music playing and everything was ready.

Ducking into the downstairs bathroom she reapplied her light pink lipstick. *Stupid Tori, you are not a contestant.* She rolled her eyes at herself. Nonetheless she patted down the wayward strands of hair until they sat flat and pinched her cheeks until colour returned. Unlike the ladies outside dressed for a cocktail party, she wore dress jeans and a white blouse. One of her favourite outfits and very comfortable, but perhaps not what she'd choose for TV.

Excited conversation became louder and the host commenced her rehearsed speech. Zac must have arrived. Exiting the bathroom she collided with Nan. 'We're on darling, all ready to go?'

Offering Nan a broad smile, she nodded. 'I'll grab a stubby from the fridge and meet you on the verandah.' Beer used to be Zac's favourite drink. Was it still?

Zac slid out of the Prado that had delivered the contestants hours before.

Her breath hitched. Had his shoulders always been so broad? Had he always filled his jeans so well? No doubt about it, Zac was one fine strapping man. His clothes appeared crisp and new. Resplendent in blue, his chambray shirt matched his dark jeans perfectly. Polished leather boots completed the outfit. Only his hair gave the slightest hint of character with his sandy blonde hair long and tousled on top, like he'd recently had a shower.

Gulp.

He stood next to the car and looked towards the deck where all eyes were trained on him. His eyes skittered back to the ground and with one hand he slammed the door shut. His other hand lay bunched to his chest, grasped there in an awkward position. The bulk of his chest rose and fell before he took a couple of tentative steps toward the house.

Zac Coleman was nervous. But wasn't this exactly what he wanted – to find love? His future wife might be standing before him. What had happened in the last few years that had caused Zac to resort to a reality dating show?

Tori assumed he'd have married long ago, maybe even to Susie and had a bunch of kids. At thirty-five, the same age as her, there'd been plenty of time for him to meet the right girl and settle down.

Perhaps all would be revealed during the taping of the show? She was the hired help anyway and it made no difference to her.

Tori was transfixed though, not unlike the contestants, as he swaggered towards them.

Expecting Zac to approach each of the women and greet them, he instead walked in the opposite direction once he reached the verandah and headed for her. What?

'Victoria.'

His voice ran like honey down her throat.

'Hmm,' she said, conscious the camera was rolling and Zac was not talking to the gorgeous women on the deck but to her instead.

He looked down at the bundle in his arms and said, 'You forgot to come and collect them, so I'm home delivering.'

Zac held Puddles and Rainbow.

Tori blinked. 'Oh, sorry,' she babbled. 'I forgot all about them with the preparations for tonight and helping Nan. Thank you, Zac. Mirabelle will be thrilled they're back and well.' She sounded formal and stiff. *Get a grip, Tori!*

Zac held them out but wasn't quick enough. One of them peed and a little trickle of urine dribbled down his shirt leaving a strong and acidic smell.

'Oh, Zac, so sorry. Now you'll stink.'

He smiled and she saw his shoulders loosen. 'Well, at least I know your guinea pigs are feeling better,' he said and handed them over.

Turning, he approached each woman. Like the good country gentleman he was, he shook their hands politely. But these women didn't appreciate his good manners and pulled him in close for a kiss instead. Zac's cheeks flushed and Tori stifled a giggle as they all avoided his urine-soaked shirt.

After the introductions, the ladies surrounded him like a school of piranha, talking rapidly, their words spilling over one another. Her nan stood to the side, grinning before gesturing for Tori to offer the drink to Zac.

She handed the pets to Nan and stepped forward, but the girls didn't let her penetrate the circle. 'Zac, would you like a drink?' Her voice rose over the top of the blathering.

All heads turned towards her and she held out the can of beer with the condensation pooling down its sides.

Zac moved through the small group and stood before her. 'Thank you.' His voice came out croaky and he cleared his throat.

Tori swallowed, her throat suddenly dry as she pushed her pesky glasses up on her nose. Zac stared hard at her and she also felt the weight of four pairs of other eyes. He paused too long. Was he going to take the drink? About to ask if he'd prefer something else, he reached for it.

'Thank you, Victoria,' he turned towards Nan too, 'and Rosalie, for hosting us. I'm glad you're here.' Then he took a large swig of the beer. Her mouth went drier as his Adam's apple bobbed.

Once again she imagined those lips on hers and her mind wandered until one of the ladies asked him a question. It snapped Tori out of her, what? Nostalgia? Lust? How ridiculous. She was fleeing a cheating husband and didn't have time for any man. And particularly not another two-timer, nor, one dating four women at once.

'I'll get the nibbles for you to enjoy with your drinks whilst watching the sun set.' Geez, now she sounded like a tour guide.

Nan gazed at her with a puzzled expression, her head titled in question. Tori moved away and Nan swiftly followed.

'You okay, dear?'

'Sure, why?'

Nan gave her a silly grin but she ignored her and busied herself preparing the platter of delights. 'These look delicious,' Nan said, but her voice was sing-songy and too high.

'I'm not sure what you're getting at, this is almost ready,' Tori sighed.

'Tell me what we have?'

'There is hummus, spring rolls, aubergine and chickpea pieces and carrot and caraway crackers to compliment.'

Tori had taste-tested everything and it was good, even if she said so herself. She'd perfected many of these recipes from catering events and the guests had loved them, so she hoped tonight wouldn't be any different.

'I'm thinking I might be able to continue my catering business whilst I'm in town. I used to do so much in Brissy. The timing is terrible because I was building a fantastic client base and now I've left.'

Nan stopped fussing over the plate. 'Tori you're a brilliant cook. Even as a child you were happiest in the kitchen baking up treats or preparing meals. I think it's fabulous to have a goal and Brisbane would have been a great market for your vegan business. This platter looks divine but let's take one step at a time and see how tonight goes.'

Nan leaned over and kissed her cheek. Tori smelled lavender talcum powder and inhaled deeply. It was her Nan's scent and transported her back to her childhood.

Laughter drifted indoors and she handed Nan the plate. 'You take this and I'll continue prepping dinner.'

5

———

Tori moved around the oblong oak table refilling the champagne flutes. It was impossible not to listen to the chatter. The host, a confident, dark-haired woman in her thirties, sat at the head of the table and acted as interviewer. She tossed out questions randomly which broke the silence and prevented awkwardness.

'So, Zac why did you sign up for the show?'

Tori paused, desperate to hear the answer. The bottle of bubbly was only half-empty, but she retrieved another from the sideboard, deliberated over popping the cork and slowed her steps. Anything to delay.

'Well,' he stammered, 'actually, I didn't sign up for the show.'

The ladies all spoke at once before the host settled them down and asked Zac to elaborate.

'My younger sisters, Holly and Lara applied and didn't tell me. The first I knew about the show was when I received a call to let me know I'd been accepted and the details for filming would be sent through to me.' He paused letting the statement sink in.

The cold bottle of Dom Perignon slipped in Tori's hand and drops of liquid spilled onto the lap of the lady seated in front of her. Clare, the country girl, dabbed at the wet spot on her dress but never took her eyes off Zac.

'But clearly,' the host continued, 'you want to find love?'

Zac glanced at each of the ladies who in turn either crossed their arms, took another sip of their drink or replaced the napkin on their lap.

'I'd love to meet a nice girl.'

Lame, Zac, lame.

There was silence, except for the sound of the cameraman sweeping the room to capture expressions before they vanished.

'And what would you say you're searching for in a partner?'

Man, the host was persistent, but it was her job after all.

Instinctively Tori glanced up, eager for his reply and their eyes connected. Her heart did a little pitter-patter in her chest. His mouth opened to speak but then Nan bustled into the room too fast and the door swung against the frame, slamming loudly and stealing away the moment. Zac jumped up to take the two plates she carried, placing them on the table. Tori distributed the fresh and still warm sourdough bread.

Saved by the bell?

The room remained quiet, the chatter commencing again after the meal was served.

'Are you vegetarian, Zac?'

He shook his head.

'Interesting. As a cattle farmer I imagined you'd love your red meat but there's no meat in this meal tonight?' asked the exotic Asian woman. Even her voice was fine, like silk.

Tori was on her way towards the kitchen with her back to Zac and the table. 'Well, firstly, I'm not a cattle farmer, but I do love steak but I eat it all the time. So I arranged something different tonight.'

That was a lie. Tori smiled and left the room.

DESSERT HAD BEEN SERVED AND THANKFULLY SHE AND NAN HAD A moment to sit on the bar stools in the kitchen, enjoying a cuppa before the clean-up.

Her body sagged with relief at the first hot sip. It was short-lived. A shrill squeal rang out, followed by a second and a third. She jumped up quicker than Nan and raced into the dining room.

'Something ran over my foot!'

'Mine too.'

'Is it a rat?'

Tori dropped to her hands and knees and scoured the floor.

'Puddles! Rainbow! Come here you pesky creatures,' she thought she whispered.

'Puddles!' Tiffany, the blonde wearing the short skirt upon arrival, jumped up and stood on her chair. 'What is it? A rodent?'

'Technically they are a breed of rodent…' Zac didn't finish the sentence before two more of the women jumped up on their chairs. Only the country chick, obviously not afraid of critters, remained seated.

Zac crouched down too. Puddles darted across the rug. 'He's under the table,' Tori yelled.

Tori crawled under one end and Zac came from the other. She shuffled backwards, checking under each chair, lifting the rim of the plaid rug. Nothing. Half-way and she bumped into Zac. Both swivelled to face the other. In the semi-darkness Tori could make out his wicked grin, his teeth all white and gleaming. A twinkle spread to his eyes and they crinkled at the edges in mischief. She sat back on her haunches and placed her hand over her mouth to stifle her giggle. Zac put one finger to his mouth urging her to be quiet.

'Are you two okay down there?' The host asked but Tori couldn't respond lest the giggles break free.

'Yep, almost got him. Stand still up there until we do.' With his grin becoming even wider, Zac lifted up a hand to reveal the runaway guinea pig securely fastened in his grip.

Tori dropped her hands and placed her palms flat on the floor. Her laughter fizzled away like the bubbles in the glasses of champagne sitting on the table. Zac sat so close, the heat radiated off his body. It mixed in with the scent of dried pee and the musty smell of hair from the bundle he held. The two of them were alone and Zac was making no effort to move. He kept staring at her as if seeing her for the first time. 'It's nice to see you again,' he said, all innocent-like, as if they weren't hiding from a roomful of women vying for his attention.

Puddles squeaked.

'I can hear it. Where is it?' one of the women shrieked.

The long tablecloth was lifted in one corner letting in the light. 'Yoo hoo under there. What's happening?' Nan sang out.

With their eyes glued to each other they both backtracked out from opposite ends of the table. Not paying attention, Tori clocked her head on the thick leg as she climbed out.

'Got him!' Zac yelled from the other end of the room. A cacophony of noise erupted and chairs scraped as bodies came back to the ground.

'Oh, it's so cute,' they exclaimed in sexy voices.

Tori rose to her feet and rubbed the bump on her head. The four women surrounded Zac petting the guinea pig.

She hoped it shit all over them.

6

<hr>

Tori stood at the washing line at the rear of the farmhouse and hung the white sheets and towels her nan had forgotten about earlier. She sent Nan to bed and insisted she'd hang the linen they needed for tomorrow's clean sheets.

An ocean of darkness surrounded her, with only the lights from the homestead to guide her. Plus, the stars. She'd forgotten about the vastness of a starry sky, its sparkling array of beauty. You never saw skies like it in the city. And a sight she must show Mirabelle.

There was something about the isolation of the country; it made you feel small and unimportant but also part of something incredibly special. Tori soaked up the contentment it provided her.

Hushed voices came from her right followed by the sound of heels on the pebbled path. She peered in that direction and saw the silhouette of a man and a woman. Even wearing her glasses she couldn't see them clearly. This path led to the cabins where the contestants were staying. Who would it be?

After the guinea pig debacle she'd departed the evening pretty quickly, not wanting to cause any more trouble. How much of the footage would make the show? She knew these productions edited and manipulated the material for prime TV viewing and hopefully it wouldn't look too bad for the B&B.

But she'd really disappeared to hide from Zac. What was that display under the table? They weren't eighteen anymore playing childhood games. But it had been kind of funny. Thinking about his mischievous grin, her tummy flipped.

The sounds moved closer and Tori hung the last sheet, collected the wash basket and moved into the darkness surrounding the house.

Long, wavy platinum blonde hair shone in the light as the couple passed by the clothesline, less than a metre from where she stood. Giggles echoed on the breeze and Tori saw Tiffany wobble on her too-high stilettos. Ridiculous footwear for the country, but she'd admit the narrow silver straps hugged her ankles nicely.

Of all the girls, Tori imagined she was the least compatible with Zac. But she didn't know the boy she went to school with anymore. Perhaps he'd changed?

Zac reached to steady Tiffany and she sought out his hand linking their fingers together and swung them to and fro. A few more steps and Tiffany yanked on Zac's arm and pulled him to a stop placing their bodies half in shadow. Ever polite, Zac paused, waiting. Tiffany stood on tiptoes and leaned in towards him.

Zac was slow to cotton on but as she neared his face, he leaned in with a swift jerky movement to plant a kiss on her cheek. 'Well, it's late and I must get you back to your cabin.' He turned and kept walking, stopping a little ahead to wait for her to catch up.

Tori gripped her sides to hold in the laughter.

Thank goodness she hadn't witnessed a passionate kiss between the pair. Talk about awkward. It gave her a bizarre sense of satisfaction that Tiffany's ploy had failed. Once Zac kissed any of these women they would be gone, hook, line and sinker. Well, that is, if he was still as good a kisser as she remembered.

And somehow, Tori imagined he would be.

'GOOD MORNING, TORI, I'M ANNA FOX, HOST AND JOURNALIST FOR the show. Last night's dinner was delicious, thank you. I'm a vegetarian too and I appreciated the food, even if it was a bit too fancy for some.' She winked at Tori. 'The producers and I are wondering if you could be the caterer. You know, obviously for all the meals here at the farmhouse, of course, but also on location. I'm not sure if you understand how the show works, but Zac will be taking each of the ladies on a date and we'd like you to provide the meals for them and the crew as well.'

Tori wiped her forearm across her brow. She was right in the midst of making savoury pancakes for breakfast and Anna spoke so fast she couldn't keep up.

'Yes, of course, I'd love to help out.'

'There's a catch. You'll need to remember your audience. After all, we feature on regional television and country folk are our main viewers. They don't want to see fancy mocked-up MasterChef food. They want locally sourced and traditional country meals.' She paused. When Tori didn't respond, she continued. 'Meat. You'll have to serve meat.' She held her fingers up to indicate inverted commas.

Oh, that was a catch. Tori hadn't cooked meat or prepared meals with dairy for, well, a long time. It went against all of her beliefs. And how could she serve that sort of food and hope to develop her vegan business? It'd be a contradiction. No, unfortunately, she couldn't help. Anna's mobile rang as she was about to refuse. Answering but holding the phone away from her ear, Anna said, 'Awesome. I'm so glad you've agreed. I'll let you know the schedule pronto!' And she left the kitchen leaving Tori with her mouth hanging open.

SHE WAS STILL WASHING THE BREAKFAST DISHES, HER HANDS IN THE sudsy water at the sink when the cameraman strode in flapping a piece of paper.

'Here's today's schedule. Last night Zac chose Lucy as his first date and they're going fishing today in that famous river of yours.'

Tori stared at him.

'Um, you know the mass of water that separates the town and is filled with fish?' he said.

'Um, Zac chose a date last night? Was it like a rose ceremony where he had to pick one and left the others hanging?'

The man smiled and Tori noticed for the first time he didn't have his camera sitting on his shoulder. 'No, different show. We can't rip them off. He chose at the end of the evening. You'd probably knocked off by then.'

Oh, yeah, sure.

'Which one is Lucy?' she asked.

'The redhead.'

Okay he'd chosen sensible shoes and active wear.

'I understand you're going to be catering and today we need a picnic for the couple to enjoy after their fishing experience.'

Yes, she could do that. Her mind immediately conjured up delicacies. Oh, no, damn, she needed *normal food*.

'Do I need to run the menu by anyone beforehand?' she asked him.

'Nah, Anna trusts you. Just make sure there's enough for me,' he laughed, 'I'm the only crew. Anna won't be on set today as there's no hosting duties. She'll voice-over later.'

They talked a bit longer, finishing with the small details and timings. Tori shook the excess water off her hands and held one out. 'By the way, I'm Tori. We haven't met properly and if we're going to work together we should at least know each other's names.'

He reciprocated and shook her hand firmly. 'Mike,' he said and walked away. 'See you in a couple of hours.'

Two hours. Shit. There was heaps of work to do. Tori prayed her nan's pantry and freezer were fully stocked. And she'd have to ask Nan to look after Mirabelle.

But Tori didn't think about the picnic. Her thoughts were on Zac.

7

───────

Zac glanced under his lashes at Lucy. He didn't feel anything other than uncomfortable.

Lucy was pretty with dramatic red hair, dimples in her cheeks and seemed to be a nice girl. He waited for fireworks to explode in his chest when she smiled at him. Nup. Nothing. Those were the dreams of movies, anyway.

But he wanted to feel a twinge of excitement ripple through him. It happened *every single time* he saw Victoria. His heart beat too fast and his mouth went dry. He wouldn't call it fireworks exactly, but it was a visceral reaction that had him gravitating towards her at any opportunity.

And man, today she wore a simple summer dress. It was thirty degrees out and she wore shoestring straps revealing bare shoulders and showing off long lithe legs. Her dark hair hung down her back and reached the hem. To him, she resembled the girl he remembered at eighteen.

So, right now, poor Lucy didn't have too much of a chance

because it took all his effort to stop staring at Victoria. But Tori was married.

She had a daughter.

Family was important.

She didn't live in *Cedar Creek Plains*.

So, basically, he was an idiot. Zac turned his body away so he couldn't see her in his peripheral vision as she set up their picnic lunch.

Time to focus on fishing and Lucy.

This river was the major feature of the town. Tall, majestic Cedars resembling Christmas trees ran for miles along each side of the banks, hence the town's name.

It was the strangest thing, those vast and open plains that crept up upon the river. During drought the grasslands were dry and brown and filled with dust. But now, after the rains, they were plentiful and lush and sometimes green, sometimes the colour of spun gold. In the middle was an oasis. A lengthy, snaking river provided the lifeblood of the community. Made it less dry and more appealing.

'Do you fish much?' he asked. Fishing was one of the most popular pastimes in the community after team sport.

'No, I've never fished. Used to watch my dad and brother do it when I was younger.'

'Okay, here's to new experiences.' Zac clinked their champagne flutes but his was empty. As if Victoria had been watching them with an eagle eye, she appeared and filled the glasses.

He was embarrassed treating her like a maid. 'Thank you...' he started to say more but looked up, noting Victoria's red and puffy eyes. He dropped his fishing rod and stood. 'What's wrong?'

She hiccupped in response, placed her hand to her mouth and walked back to the picnic spot.

He hurried after her not glancing at Lucy. Zac placed his hand to the small of her back. Through the thin cotton fabric he felt the knuckles of her spine.

'Zac. You're on your date. Don't worry about me. I'm fine. I had a call from my husband and well, um, he's a jerk.'

He pulled her in close and cradled her head against his chest, one hand to her moist cheek and held tight. Inhaling her honey and vanilla scent, he closed his eyes a moment too long. Time and place got lost until the clearing of a throat.

Shit. He pulled away but gawped at Victoria. Her misery was like a physical pain deep in his gut. A raw and primitive urge overtook him; to protect her, keep her safe and happy, dry her tears and murmur reassurances. Instead Victoria moved away and fussed with the picnic. Dismissed, Zac turned back to the riverbank and Lucy. His arms ached to have her back in his embrace.

What the hell was wrong with him?

He had to pull himself together. Reaching Lucy, he pushed out the words, 'So sorry. I've known Victoria since we were kids and she's upset about something back at home.'

At that moment his rod bent. 'Lucy, a fish,' he laughed and pointed. 'Reel it in.' Lucy picked up the pole and held it in the air. It jerked in her hands before bouncing towards the bank and out of her grip. Zac ran after the rod and grasped it before working furiously to save the fish he'd hooked. Lucy squealed as the splashes of water wet her clothes and even louder when the fish finally landed on the earth.

'Oh, that's disgusting. It's bleeding, Zac because the hook is caught in its mouth. Throw it back in,' she demanded.

Zac stared at the fish and didn't respond to Lucy.

It was a solid catch of legal length and he wanted to keep it.

After a pause, Zac threw the fish into the river after

extracting the hook. 'Let's have lunch.' He pulled his lips into a tight smile.

'Oh, this is beautiful. How perfect. Thank you, Zac.' Lucy leaned over and kissed him, like he'd set up the checked picnic blanket with low set table and a vase of wildflowers and a candle that refused to stay lit. Platters of finger sandwiches and quiches lined the table, along with jugs of sparkling cold water.

Victoria stood near the SUV packing something away. Lucy talked. He tried to concentrate, he really did, but her voice droned on. Then out of the corner of his eye he saw Victoria fall to the ground where she lay motionless. Zac dropped his glass, the liquid spilling all over the place as he jumped up and raced over. The camera loomed in his face.

'She's fainted. Get some water.'

Without releasing the camera, Mike rushed to Lucy who remained on the rug mopping up the mess. She silently poured a glass of mineral water and Mike rushed back, the liquid slopping over the lip.

Zac shook Victoria but she didn't respond. He slapped her cheeks until she roused and moved her up into a sitting position. She pushed his hands away.

'Get back to your date,' she said through gritted teeth.

'Let me get you something to drink and eat and ensure you're okay.'

Zac rushed over to the picnic and collected a handful of goodies in a napkin Lucy prepared for him. He offered her a smile of apology. 'Be back in a tic.' Lucy shrugged.

'Zac I can't eat any of this food. I prepared the chicken and watercress, and egg and lettuce sandwiches for you and Lucy.'

'Oh, okay. What about some custard tart or a sugar rush with a square of chocolate?'

Again, she shook her head.

'You don't eat your own food?'

Victoria stood and he placed his hand under her elbow, supporting her. Slowly she took tentative steps away towards the shade and a camping chair.

'I'm queasy. I'm going to sit for a moment and have a drink. I'm probably dehydrated. It's warm today although the sun is losing some of its heat. Anyway, you need to take Lucy for a lovely walk along the riverbank and devote yourself to whatever it is she wants to talk about. Whether it's the latest fashion, movies or osteo technique.'

'Osteo technique?'

'She's an osteopath, Zac. Geez. Pay attention. Get it?'

Her gaze seared into him. She was right of course; he was being disrespectful. His sisters would be ashamed of him. He was ashamed of himself but there was no way he wouldn't have helped when she'd collapsed. But now he had to do the right thing. The only way to do that was to be far away from Victoria and near Lucy.

Zac nodded. Why then did his heart feel so heavy in his chest?

8

———————

Tori had to admit she loved watching *The Bachelor*; had watched each season. There was something about observing two people fall in love. The romantic in her enjoyed the intimacy of it, but not so much the gossip and dramatics. The producers were clever at delivering good television. It worked though, because people were glued to the screen.

But *Local Lads Looking for Love* was not *The Bachelor*.

Anna and the crew seemed to make up the rules as they went along. As best Tori could work out, similar scenarios were playing out in nearby regional towns. Other Aussie blokes were hosting four contestants in their hometown and escorting them on dates. Occasionally, like tonight, they would have a hook-up to share stories and check on progress and, hopefully hear a country-boy had fallen in love.

Unlike the national show where there were numerous dates and contestants all vying for the attention of the bachelor, the regional show allowed for only one date with each lady. Otherwise, they spent time eating dinners together and similar to a camp atmosphere, they might play games or host a Q&A. All with Zac as the special guest of course.

Rumour (from Mike) was that Zac could send a woman home at any time.

Yesterday after her fainting episode, she'd devoured a generous slice of the custard tart she'd made for the picnic. It was part nostalgia and part desperation. It was Nan's recipe and she'd made it religiously with Tori as a child. It had been Pop's favourite too.

Tori remembered many occasions sitting on the kitchen barstool as her nan worked her magic. Her grandmother had nurtured her love of cooking and being back home with her was making Tori happier than she'd expected. Despite her unfaithful husband and her heart being shattered into a million pieces, each time Nan cuddled her or helped in the kitchen, she felt healed.

But Tori hadn't eaten a tart or any sort of pastry for more than ten years. It had been a trip down memory lane making the treat: rolling out the sugar-laden base, beating the eggs and stir-ring the boiling custard. Like the old days it had turned out beautifully; a classic country dish.

If she'd returned to the past baking it, taking the first slice was metamorphic. There'd been an explosion of taste she'd long forgotten and it had delivered other childhood memories. Many of them contained a young Zac.

Anyway, the ridiculously delicious treat had landed her back to earth with a thump with the past and present colliding. It didn't take away her nausea, however, the sick feeling settled in the base of her stomach today.

Tonight she'd cooked two of her favourite dishes: orecchiette with cream and carrot miso sauce and vegan alfredo. The guinea pigs were locked up and she, Nan and Mirabelle ate in the kitchen, leaving the game show to play out in the living room.

Like Tori did as a child, Mirabelle shadowed her nan.

'Did you feed the chickens today?'

'Yes,' she said, 'and the little piggy. Oink, oink,' she imitated.

The three generations laughed together.

'What's next for the show?' her nan asked.

'Tomorrow night is some sort of Q&A thingo where questions are thrown at Zac. There's a cardboard box in the living room where the contestants can anonymously ask him questions, presumably contentious ones if they are too shy to ask him directly!'

'That sounds fun. We'll have to tune in,' her nan said delighted and clapped her hands.

'The next big date is an overnight camping adventure on Zac's property. A bit awkward because I'll be there with Zac, his date and Mike. I'll be in the background of course, but it was totally weird the other day serving up lunch while they're trying to get to know each other.'

'It might not have been so strange if you hadn't fainted and distracted Zac.' Nan laughed.

'Don't joke, Nan, it was terrible. Lucy sat on the picnic rug alone while Zac was busy slapping me on the face.' Nan broke out in raucous chuckles, prompting Mirabelle to join in.

'Well it sounds pretty tame tonight,' Tori commented. Not a sound emanated from the dining room. 'Why don't you catch an early night and I'll clean up?'

Nan placed her wrinkly brown hand over hers. 'Gosh, it's lovely having you back, Tori.' Nan's eyes misted. 'Thank you for all of your help.' The old woman turned to Mirabelle. 'I'll tuck you up in bed while Mummy finishes and we'll read two books.'

'Ten books!' Mirry squealed.

Tori knew Mirry would sucker Nan into reading way more than she intended.

BEFORE THE QUESTIONS HAD EVEN BEGUN, THE LADIES WERE DRUNK. She supposed it was on purpose but Tori noticed Anna remained sober.

And Zac, well he kept to himself not sitting near any of the women but nursing a stubby and chatting with Nan.

'Okay, Zac,' Anna's voice was too loud and Tori grimaced. The woman's hand was in the box and she extracted a small square of paper. 'First question – what is your idea of a romantic night out?'

'A night at the pub?'

'Ah, c'mon, Zachary Coleman,' Anna shouted. 'You can do better.'

Zac blushed and bowed his head, confronted over taking the lazy option.

'Enjoying a moonlit dinner under the stars with good food and wine, and of course wonderful company.'

'Well, Zac. That's more like it. What do you think, ladies?' They made appropriate comments.

'Zac, you're a handsome country lad. Why is it you haven't settled down before now?' Anna asked the next question and before Zac could answer she said, 'Great questions, ladies!'

Tori held her breath. This was her question. She'd snuck it into the box when no one was watching. She'd been dying to ask since she'd first run into Zac. Why was he single?

Zac heaved a big sigh like he was tired of the interrogation already. More likely, he preferred staying out of the spotlight. She'd always known him to be a private person.

There's nowhere to hide, Zac.

'Um, there isn't any exciting answer to this one. I simply haven't met the right girl.' He sat back defiant, not prepared for challenge on this answer.

Rubbish. Tori didn't buy it. He was being coy and secretive. There had to be more to it and she determined to find out the real answer.

'Righteo,' Anna trilled and grinned down the camera lens. 'Toilet seat up or down?' The ladies erupted in laughter.

'Down of course. I have four sisters.'

The ladies clapped.

'Next one – a bit more serious. Tell us about your relationship with your mother and your family.'

Zac took a gulp of beer. 'My mum is a strong, no nonsense practical woman who is a saint for putting up with the shenanigans of my sisters and my grumpy father.'

Tori remembered his mother as a model country wife. Running the household while her husband managed the cattle property. She'd always been welcomed with home-baked afternoon teas and a smile. Plus, his sisters were always such great fun. To her, his loud and rambunctious family had been a great diversion from her non-existent one. She knew Zac felt differently.

'Do all of your sisters still live locally?' Anna interjected.

'Yes in the country. They don't all live in *Cedar Creek Plains*, but close by.'

Anna nodded. Zac was being a bit of a killjoy and the mood turned sombre.

'Let's keep going then shall we. We're loving getting to know you better, Zac.'

Tori sat glued to her seat at the rear of the living room, resting her feet up after another long day. The house could burn down around her and she'd stay to devour each word Zac revealed about himself even in his modest terms.

Anna raced through more jovial questions. Favourite colour – green. Animal – all of them. Food – steak.

None of them revealed much about the true Zac, but kept the contestants entertained and no doubt the audiences at home too.

Zac finished his second beer. 'Okay. It's been fun getting to know our resident Lad but here's our last question for the evening and it's a goodie. Zac, have you ever been in love?'

There was no hesitation. Zac's eyes roamed the room until they found her. The gap between them lessened while all of the air sucked out of the room. Tori shifted her feet off the seat in front and sat up with a straight back, one hand holding the tea. Suddenly, the mug she held with its cartoon design held her attention. Only fleetingly though. She couldn't avoid the pull of his stare. When she glanced back, his magnetic eyes zeroed in on her. It was impossible to look away. There was no twinkle tonight or creased lines shadowing his eyes from a smile that stretched too far. The moment dragged and Tori sucked in a breath.

One of the women turned in her seat. Another took a sip of her drink. Tori heard Anna breathing into the microphone. But it was like no one else was in the room, only her and Zac. She wasn't supposed to be in the spotlight. Little beads of sweat rolled down her chest.

Finally he broke the contact. 'Yes,' he said, 'a long time ago.'

The theme song to the show erupted and the scene, like one in a movie, ended. Mike moved in too close with the camera, but Zac shoved him away and rose to leave the room.

'Who wants another drink?' Clare asked.

9

Tori wasn't required at the camping site while Zac and Sophie set up their tents. In fact, she'd rather be skinning a goat than be hanging around like a voyeur. But there were only two cars and she travelled with Mike who had to capture every minute of the action.

Zac chose the grand sweeping plains of his sizeable family property for the overnight adventure. He'd also chosen Sophie, the exotic and alluring woman. If he chose a partner based on elegance and beauty, Sophie was that girl.

Tori grabbed the front of her shirt and puffed it out a few times to catch a breeze. It was great to spend most days in these clothes again. She mightn't look as fancy as Sophie but it was comfortable and practical. Except for those bloody flies. Them she would never like.

A cow bellowed in the near distance. A small herd of deep red cattle were bunched under a copse of shady trees. Some rubbed their necks together, others lazed on the ground. Their musty manure scent drifted towards her.

Her mind drifted to her husband and what he might be doing now. Had the Pilates instructor moved into their home? Once again she wondered where it all went wrong. She'd been a good wife she'd thought. Did men require more? Or did they bore easily?

Tori stole a glance at Zac. He seemed so different – caring, genuine, every girl's best friend. But then he'd kissed her while dating Susie. So, yeah, they might all be the same.

Thinking about her cheating husband no longer made her sick. Instead a ball of fury swirled in her chest. How dare he do that to her. How dare he ruin their marriage; their family life; not be an available father for Mirabelle? One thing she refused to do was blame herself. She wasn't the one having sex with someone else. That was him. All him. She was not responsible for his behaviour. And because he couldn't keep it in his pants. No, maybe she did feel a bit sick after all.

There had been a mixture of emotions returning to *Cedar Creek Plains* but also resolve. She could make it on her own; start a successful business and provide for Mirabelle. She didn't need Todd or any man to care for her. Tori Christensen could damn well look after herself.

Tori stood tall and stretched out her back. The horizon went as far as she could see, well past the cows and the boundary fences. In the distance, some kilometres away sat the Coleman family homestead. She could make out the main house and the surrounding stables and sheds. In front, the long flat plains supported tiny tufts of grass, their new growth swaying in a breeze so gentle it hardly kissed her skin. She wiped her forearm across her brow, the scorching sun was biting her bare skin.

Tori set up her make-shift kitchen under the nearest tree. Dinner prep was done and she needed to pitch her own tent before dark.

Heading over to the car she saw two tents circling a fire pit with matching camping chairs. Would the couple be using one tent tonight?

Zac stood to the side of the car and pitched another tent.

Her tent.

'Hey, what are you doing?'

'Oh, hey. Just setting this up for you. I'm sure Mike isn't going to do it.'

'Nor does he have to, or you. I'll do it.' She walked closer and took the canvas top out of his hands. He let her take it without a word and she draped it over the tent's canopy. Zac hammered in the corner pegs before saluting and heading back to Sophie.

When he was about half-way across, a flock of birds took off in fright and filled the cloudless sky. Zac whipped out his phone and angled it above him. He examined the shots and stood still for a moment staring at his phone.

'I'll finish this and bring over the esky and cool drinks,' she shouted to his departing back. He waved in acknowledgement.

Tori lugged over the heavy esky while Mike filmed.

'Mike, are you married?'

'Nuh.'

'Hmm,' Tori commented.

'Hey, what's that supposed to mean?'

'Nothing.'

When she arrived at the cosy site, Zac was on his mobile, listening and nodding.

Tori extracted a bottle of chilled champagne and two glasses. She indicated to Sophie who nodded.

Zac ended his call. His right hand crept up the back of his neck and rubbed his hair line. 'I'm so sorry, Sophie,' he said but glanced in Tori's direction. 'There's a vet emergency. A horse has gone into labour and is having difficulty. The farmer's worried the foal might be stuck. I have to go. I'll make it up to you, I promise and be as fast as I can.'

'Zac,' Tori said, 'what about the Chief. Is he still away?'

Zac nodded confirmation as he rushed to the car.

Tori turned to Sophie. 'The man he works with is away on holiday and Zac is the only vet in town and for miles. He wouldn't go if he didn't have to. Here have a drink.'

Sophie didn't respond but accepted the drink and downed it in one swallow. Not so elegant after all. Tori refilled it and was about to pour her own and pull up a chair when Sophie rose and marched towards her tent.

Zac wouldn't be long, she was sure. Knowing him, the guilt at leaving would spur him on to act as quickly as possible; he'd feel dreadful.

Tori busied herself with dinner. This time Mike had remained and not followed to film the action. 'Enough footage of vetting,' he muttered as he cracked open a can of beer.

The sun sank lower to meet the horizon. It was one of the best times of day in the country. Time for supper. She served Mike a bowl of simple beef stew. She'd gone out of her comfort zone to create a life-like camping experience. A lot of good it had done. Sophie hadn't come out of her tent, so Tori made knock-knock noises and served her the meal inside. 'Mike and I are sitting by the fire if you'd like to join us.' Sophie replied with a tight smile but didn't follow.

Zac returned over two hours later. The light was out in Sophie's tent and he didn't rouse her. Tori remained by the fire, enjoying the peace and quiet of country life.

'Sit down. You must be starving. I'll get your dinner.'

Mike had collapsed in the driver's seat of the car where his body hung over the steering wheel, snoring. He hadn't even bothered to set up his tent.

Tori handed over the steaming plate. 'I must say your track record with these dates isn't great.' She laughed, sat down and got them both a drink. Zac rolled the can of beer over his forehead and down his cheeks, puffing them out as he enjoyed the cool metal on his face.

'Don't laugh. These poor girls. Here they are waiting for these romantic interludes with jackass old me and it's all turned to shit.' He took a big swig of beer.

'Not your fault.'

'I know. But circumstance, right?' He spooned a couple of mouthfuls of stew in quick succession. 'Oh, this is incredible. Thank you.'

'You don't like my usual vegan, vegetarian, dairy free fare?'

Zac held up a palm in defeat. 'I didn't say that. In fact the meals we've had at your nan's have been outstanding. But I've been raised on traditional tucker. What is it with that food anyway? You never used to be vegetarian.'

'I'm vegan. Don't eat meat or any meat-based products, including eggs and cheeses etcetera.'

'Man, you're missing out. I love a slather of cheese spread over a cracker…'

Tori relaxed and slumped into the chair, leaning back. The stars twinkled at her like diamonds in the sky. 'It was a gradual thing. There is so much on offer in the city – five different varieties of coffee, and milk. Every plausible food you can think of – Thai, Indian, Lebanese and shops devoted solely to chocolates or French pastries; anything you can think of. I worked a few odd jobs here and there and tasted each of those foods. It was heaven. I joined a gym not too long after and met Todd.'

'Your husband?'

She nodded. 'He owned and ran the gym. I was exercising a lot and losing weight and feeling great. He needed help in the gym shop and it served healthy food. You know I enjoy cooking and baking. I always have.'

He agreed in between chewing.

'I experimented and made my own healthy treats. It was so easy and so much better than that sugar-laden rubbish we shove into our bodies. I developed a small range and then branched into salads and super-foods. It's all the rage in the city. But I guess, before I could blink, I was married and my entire life had altered from the one I used to know.'

'But why did you leave in the first place?'

10

———

Her lips pressed together in a slight grimace and her gaze turned away, looking out into the dark distance. Tori uncrossed her legs and remained silent.

Had he offended her? It was a valid question. Running away without a good-bye after all the time they'd spent together growing up. And after that kiss.

He had almost given up on her response when she spoke.

'Zac, you kissed me at graduation while you were dating my best friend. I kissed you back! You cheated on Susie and I let you. I couldn't live with myself. Plus, you were convinced country living was for you. You never wanted more. I did.'

His last mouthful of beer spat from his mouth. 'Shit, sorry. That's gross. You're wrong.' He repeated, 'You're wrong. You never gave me a chance to explain. Yes, I kissed you. It was one of the best kisses I've ever experienced. And before we'd even pulled apart you ran away. Like a child.' He swallowed. He needed another sip of beer to moisten his mouth.

Tori leaned forward resting her elbows on her knees, but he kept talking. There was no way he'd let her interrupt this time.

'And didn't just run from me. You left town. I thought I'd let you cool off for a while and we'd talk the next day. That I could tell you...' He shook his head and checked out the dark horizon, taking solace in the silence and the vast openness engulfing them.

'Yes, I'd been dating Susie, but I broke up with her that night. I only had eyes for you and it wasn't fair. I kissed you after I'd told her.'

'You broke up with Susie and then kissed me?' Her voice was a whisper. A pause. 'Shit. I'm sorry. I didn't know. I'd betrayed her and I couldn't face her or you. We'd done the wrong thing.'

'Everything might have been different if you'd let me explain.'

Tori sat back and he was sure heat radiated off her and not from the raging fire. 'You think?'

Sarcasm dripped off her words. Yes, he wanted to scream. Instead, he waited for her to digest the information.

'You were destined to take over the cattle farm and live a happy country life. I wanted more. Still do, I guess, but maybe the definition has changed. So regardless, even if you'd tried to convince me to stay, I would have left eventually.'

He drank the words in. 'But now you're back.'

She cackled like there was poison in her mouth. 'I had no choice. My husband cheated on me and I fled. I have no money and nowhere else to go to get my shit together. I have responsibilities; a daughter. Thank goodness for Nan. I needed to take Mirabelle somewhere safe.'

'Was he violent?'

'No. Just a lying cheating prick.' She turned her full gaze on him. 'All these years I thought you were a cheater too. In retrospect I should've realised. You were such a nice bloke, everyone's best friend. It didn't make sense you'd do that. It upset me again when I first arrived. Brought all those memories back. I didn't stay in touch with Susie after I left because I felt so guilty. What a waste.'

Victoria shook her head; her wavy long hair fell, hiding her face. 'What *have* you done since then?'

Her voice was less friendly, exasperated maybe.

'Dad is still pressuring me to take over the cattle farm. The precious lineage. He tolerated my vet studies, said it was a valuable asset to the station. Saving money on animal husbandry. What a coup. He tolerated it less when I returned and worked with the Chief. Even then he hoped it was a passing fad. It wasn't. My dream is to buy the vet clinic off the Chief when he retires. That is what I want.'

'Wow. So you do have ambition. I'm impressed.'

The comments hurt. He'd always had ambition, but Victoria wasn't here, didn't know. He wasn't the hick country boy she remembered. 'The war wages on between us. No real urgency I guess while Dad is fit to run the station. I was laid up, off track for a while…'

He paused, collected himself before he could continue. Took a sip of his beer but the can was empty. Tori got up and pulled another from the esky.

'You don't have to serve me.'

'Well, I do actually. I'm paid to cater for your show and it's part of the job description.' Zac didn't agree and gave her a glare that said so with a shake of his head. He opened the can and drank before continuing.

'I was diagnosed with cancer a few years back. Had treatment, chemo. I'm in remission now and all clear but it was a bit stressful at the time.'

'Zac! I'm so sorry. I never knew.'

He shrugged. It was old news but he had to admit it still affected him. The experience had changed his view on life. Made him realise what he wanted and what he could achieve. In a cruel twist of fate, choices were taken from him too.

And yet, despite his close call with the game of life, what had he actually accomplished? Perhaps the best was still to come. He wouldn't admit it to her. Tori would think he was still a naïve country boy.

A loud snort emanated from the SUV where the door remained ajar. They both laughed.

'It seems as if we have both lived a lifetime. Grown up, hey?'

Zac agreed.

'But why the show, Zac. It's not your style. Surely there are a queue of girls lining up to date one of the most eligible men in town. You don't need to resort to reality TV.'

'My sisters signed me up!' he said in defence.

'I know but you're doing it. I'm sure you could've gotten out of it.'

'You know my sisters, right? They would have had my guts for garters and other parts of my anatomy too.' He let his words hang, hoping they might be enough. Not for Tori. 'Yeah, but seriously. It's for them. To shut them up for a while about me getting married and what not. Maybe it's time?'

'You've had girlfriends since?'

'Yeah, but honestly nothing serious. Few dates.' He shrugged but that didn't sum up how he felt about it at all.

'Zac Coleman. Are you telling me since Susie, you've not had a relationship?'

He didn't answer. Stared at her until she broke their hold.

Then he gazed at the stars and the moon. It provided a silvery glow on everything in its path.

Tori rose and collected the dirty plates and glasses. Zac drained his beer and followed her to the kitchen. A wild dog barked nearby and Tori jumped. They stood so close she bumped into him and he took the opportunity to hold her arm, reassure her. She turned her head towards him and he didn't drop his grip. The barking receded into the distance and the only sound was the drone of Mike's snoring.

Zac felt her take a deep breath and her chest rise and fall. Tori's body moved sideways until their torsos met and her hips brushed his. Her hot breath smelt of champagne and berries as it blew against his cheek. They both leaned their heads in, hesitating briefly until their lips connected. It was like coming home. Tori's lips were soft and warm and delicate. Zac shut his eyes as their mouths danced together, moving apart and back with kisses as tender and light as the summer breeze. His confidence grew by her hungry response and he pressed harder, his mouth devouring hers and forcing it open with his thrusting tongue. One hand entangled the hair at the nape of her neck and the other rested to her hip, his thumb grazing the waistband of her jeans. The feel of her bare flesh under his finger sent currents of desire to his core. With that one finger, he drew her body closer, her breasts resting against his chest. His knee nudged in between her legs. He was being transported. Finally, back to the lips he'd never stopped thinking about. The girl he'd once loved.

Tori placed a hand to his chest and pushed him back hard. His dream slipped away as she shoved him with her weight.

She stared at him, her pink and swollen lips parted. He lowered his head for more, but Tori took a step backwards creating space between them. Their bodies no longer touched and he ached for her already.

'You are a cheater. No different to my husband. You're dating four women on a reality show, Zac,' she hissed his name through gritted teeth. 'You have four potential women one of whom you'll pick to possibly marry one day. You cannot be kissing me. It isn't fair to them, or to me. It isn't right!'

'Shit,' he said and hung his head, raking his fingers through his hair. He kept it long for moments like these, he guessed. There'd been a few of them.

'These women ...'

'Stop. Don't offer excuses. You're committed to the show and to them until you send them home. Don't justify your actions. I thought you were different. But that proves how stupid I am. How bad I am at trusting people. The wrong people. Or maybe it's men in general. You're all a bunch of lying cheats.'

'Tori, c'mon.' He reached for her, desperate to stop her fleeing, to feel her skin once more. To hold her. It didn't work and she backed away as if he repulsed her. He flinched as she flung the remaining dirty dishes into the plastic bucket filled with water and stormed off.

11

'M**ummy!'** Mirabelle skipped towards her, the rose-pink dress she wore swinging as she moved, her unsuitable white patent shoes squeaking on the floorboards.

'I missed you so much!' Tori squeezed her too tight, relishing the squish of her baby folds. She released her daughter and said, 'This morning I have to do some cooking for tonight's dinner but when I'm finished would you like to go horse riding?'

Mirry's eyes opened wide. It was the one thing Mirry had been begging to do since they'd arrived. Tori had put her off too many times.

'Lovely, dear. Your old gear will be in the stables. It'll need a good clean I imagine,' Nan commented from the corner where she sat sipping her morning coffee.

Mirry hugged her fiercely and squealed yes, many times over. Horse riding had been one of Tori's favourite activities as a child. She'd had her own horse whom she'd adored and endless summer days to roam paddocks. The idea of riding out on isolated tracks and brushing the tips of the branches as you passed by, sent a wave of excitement rolling through her. They'd both waited too long. And after last night she desperately wanted to reconnect with passions she'd once enjoyed. And maybe with her old self?

This morning she'd risen early and set up breakfast before waking Mike and telling him she was taking the car back. She was good at running away, knew it was immature, but it was also liberating. Making her own choices. She didn't want to face Zac, not yet anyway. Tori needed distance to collect her thoughts. And Zac needed to spend time with Sophie before they headed back to the homestead. That was only fair.

A gamut of emotion pulsed through her. She wasn't angry even though she'd made him think that. Frightened and confused more accurate.

He'd broken up with Susie and then kissed her. She'd tossed and turned all night remembering those words. One thing Tori couldn't work out is what it meant. Had he liked her back then? Wanted more but she'd run away?

She'd enjoyed the kiss. Too much. And that scared her. A lot. It was like she remembered. Damn, Zac Coleman was a good kisser.

She'd accused him of being a cheater, but he wasn't. He hadn't been all those years ago either and he wasn't now. Zac was the one man she felt comfortable with. He was like a warm blanket being draped around your shoulders on a cold winter's night. Remembering those lips on hers sent shivers racing up her spine.

'Why don't you change out of those party shoes and go and feed the animals with Nan? Then you might like to sit here at the kitchen bench and do some drawing while I cook. I can't bear to be away from you a second longer.' Mirry rolled her eyes but tugged off her shoes, replacing them with wellington boots. It hadn't taken her long to adjust to the routine of the country.

Mirry's small hand clasped Nan's, their fingers entwined as they wandered out to the yard together. Tori's heart swelled. The unconditional love for a child was something else. Despite the disastrous situation of her marriage, she loved being a mother.

Focus, Tori. First, she needed to whip up a feast for tonight, suitable for a buffet, she decided because the urge to make herself scarce weighed heavily on her mind.

Tori didn't think twice about making good old-fashioned chicken pie given her tolerance to meat had grown considerably.

Talking with Zac about the past had reignited something within and she yearned for the comfort of tradition. Horse riding, and more cooking. Zac had reminded her of what she once was. She was still that person, wasn't she?

But she'd repressed many memories. How could she? They were her childhood highlights. Cooking with Nan for starters. In the early days when she'd missed her mother so much it felt like her heart was split in two, they'd spend hours in the kitchen with Nan taking her with pain-staking care through each step of a recipe.

The house had always been filled with inviting aromas and they'd shared the thrill of anticipation as their favourite creations were lifted out of the oven.

Had she gotten so way-laid with fancy super-foods like kale and spinach and quinoa and fast-spinning blenders that she'd forgotten real food was nutritious. You couldn't get much healthier than direct from a vegetable patch and organic chicken from your neighbour down the road. Pastry made from scratch had no preservatives or nasty chemicals.

Warmth spread through her body. More longing for the past but also, what? Contentment? Realisation at rediscovering her roots? No, it was hope she felt and the emotion stole her breath away, catching her by surprise.

The facts were harsh and she couldn't hide them: her marriage was over; she was broke; had a floundering vegan catering business and was currently sponging off her nan. And yet, being in the kitchen, like the small child she'd once been, and feeling the same sense of accomplishment, allowed her to feel certain everything would be okay.

It had to be. Tori pushed aside thoughts of Zac. The man was dating four women. There was hardly any cause for Tori to get her knickers in a knot. She had to get her own life back on track. *Even if* he liked her all those years ago, and there was a hint of attraction between them now...

Hours later Tori led Mirry on a narrow track heading towards the river. She inhaled the scent of her first love, her horse Giddy Up. His musty earthy smell was so familiar to her. A smell she'd always loved, but today, her stomach churned as she controlled a cramp of nausea. Tori reached for the water bottle on the side of her pack and Giddy Up nuzzled her, demanding a pat. She swallowed the cool water and rubbed his nose. He'd always been an obedient and tame horse, but now with his advanced age he was perfect for Mirry.

This life was enough. Her future could be the farm, like Nan. After Pop had died her nan had lived a full and happy life alone. Yes, she'd had customers to care for and the hobby farm to keep her busy, but Tori could be the same. She'd help out more and make a serious effort to get the business off the ground and make a success of it. She'd provide for Mirry without the help of Todd, and her daughter could grow up a country kid like she had.

Thinking about men … Despite her self-talk, she couldn't get Zac off her mind. Her belly tightened into knots remembering the words they'd exchanged. But then she recalled the kiss and her insides turned to liquid dissolving those same knots. Tori remembered the sensation; his thumb on her bare back, the feel of his body against her.

Shaking her head, she chased those thoughts away. It was the nostalgia of being home. That's all. Zac was *Cedar Creek Plains*. The two went together.

Zac was the perfect friend, had always been there for her. They could continue being great friends.

12

———

Saturday night in Cedar Creek Plains and there was only one place to be: the pub.

The lifeblood of any small town was the local. And that is exactly why Zac had chosen this as his date with Clare.

Plus, Saturday night was trivia and was always a hoot.

Clare was the perfect candidate. Zac resisted the urge to headbutt himself. Talking about candidates made it sound like he was interviewing her to be his vet assistant. That was sort of the problem though, his heart didn't flutter and his skin didn't erupt in goosebumps around Clare, or any of the women. Well, except one and she wasn't in the running.

Clare was a jillaroo. A country girl born and bred and he admired her calm demeanour and no holds barred attitude. She'd mixed in well with the other girls and could talk about anything ranging from make-up and hair which interested some of them, to horses and agriculture and the future of farming. On paper, she was his perfect woman.

She sat across from him and nursed her beer with a genuine

smile. Music blared from the rock band in the corner making talking difficult. He leaned in close to chat and their shoulders touched.

Zac focused on her dark hair pulled severely back into a bun, her distinct high cheek bones and the dark mole upon her upper lip. He checked out her eyelashes too, anything to avoid glancing across the room to where Tori sat with friends.

Mike filmed as always and the locals relished the chance to be on TV.

Mayor Graham tested the mic, asking people to group into teams of six as trivia would commence in ten minutes. Two people rushed to join their table and when elderly resident, Francine, wandered past, Zac nabbed her too. She was infamous for her general knowledge on movies, pop stars and TV from reading trashy magazines. The old woman giggled and pulled herself gingerly onto the spare stool.

The Mayor wandered the room checking on numbers and asking team names. 'Are you being shy?' he yelled into his mic. 'Here is our resident bachelor Zac with his lovely date, Clare. They need another team member folks. C'mon, who is going to volunteer? Might guarantee you a spot on the telly!' The crowd roared but no one moved.

'Here's the perfect addition to any team,' the Mayor continued. 'Welcome home, Tori. Lovely to have you back. Let's hope it's for good.' The Mayor bailed her up as she stood in line at the bar. Zac's senses went on high alert.

'Come and join the *Local Lads Looking for Love* team. They've got Francine and are sure to be in with a chance!' The crowd cheered again and raised their glasses in a toast.

Tori shook her head, her loose hair swishing around her shoulders.

Zac couldn't help but drink in the sight of her. Those long, lean legs were in faded blue jeans with slight heels giving her some height. She wore a transparent loose white blouse so he could see the swell of her breasts. He flicked his tongue across his lips and took a sip of beer. God damn.

He'd tried his best to clear the air and talk to Tori since the campout. She hadn't brushed him off exactly; she'd been evasive and polite. Acted as if everything was normal. But nothing could be normal, could it, after that kiss? It was all he could think about since. For him, the flame he'd harboured all those years ago flared brightly and continued to simmer. Unfortunate, given the circumstances he found himself in. Of all the timing for him to be coerced into a reality dating TV show.

But it was all for the best.

The Mayor droned on and Zac turned back to Clare. 'Tell me about your family.' Clare was an only child who was estranged from her parents and lived alone on an outback station. Short and simple, she said. Nothing like his large and noisy family whom he argued with regularly, but loved dearly.

Clare reached out her hand and placed it on top of his. Out of the corner of his eye, he saw Tori being bustled into position at their table. His eyes were trained on the hand that had obvious sun damage but painted pink nails. With Tori approaching on one side and Clare being intimate in the rowdy pub, his heart accelerated.

It was all shades of awkward.

Clare leaned in. 'I have to tell you up front that I do not want children.' She lowered her head closer to his and his long fringe brushed her forehead. It was intimate, wrong. 'For a relationship to work, there has to be honesty. It's important you know because I won't change my mind. I understand if my view changes the situation for you, but you need to know.' Clare withdrew her hand and placed it in her lap.

Tori sat down next to him and her leg brushed his thigh. The song playing ramped up to its crescendo and thumped too loud in his ears.

The music stopped as abruptly as it started and Mayor Graham was back on the mic announcing the trivia categories.

Clare was perfect on paper and in other respects too. It didn't bring him any joy though as he sat squashed between her and Tori in the noisy pub. All of a sudden he wanted to be anywhere but there.

THE TOILET CUBICLE DOOR OPENED AS TORI SHOOK THE WATER FROM her hands.

'Clare, I'm so sorry. I never meant to crash your date with Zac. I keep popping up but it's never my intention.'

Clare stared at her reflection in the mirror and washed her hands. 'Are you sorry?' She turned and ripped off some paper towel and threw it in the bin before facing her. 'What is it between you and Zac?'

'What do you mean?'

'Are you dating?'

'No! Zac is on the show and is dating all four of you. Not me.'

'Are you sure you're not a secret contestant that is going to surprise us in week four and run away with the prize?'

'No!'

'So, what is it then? Unrequited love? I understand you grew up together. Is there passion that hasn't been sated?' She smirked. 'Because personally I'd rather know than waste my time.'

'No, completely innocent I assure you. We were friends and ran around in the same group together.'

Clare leaned one hip against the basin as another woman entered the bathroom. She crossed her arms against her chest. 'Not buying it, Tori. The chemistry between the two of you when you're in the same room is palpable. Are you telling me you can't feel it?'

Tori went mute momentarily but found her strength and stood taller. This woman was ballsy and straight to the point but Tori wasn't intimidated. This was a reality TV show and each of these women wanted to win. It was a game after all. Who wouldn't want to win Zac's heart?

'Nah. Nothing going on. Good mates is all.'

'If you say so.' But Clare stared too hard for too long and shrugged as she dawdled towards the door, shoulders back, hips swaying. A waft of her perfume clung to the air and tickled Tori's nose. The taste lay on her tongue and lined her throat. She gagged. Bile burned before Tori clasped her hand over her mouth and rushed back to the nearest toilet. She only had time to lift the lid before vomiting.

Despite multiple rinses she couldn't rid her mouth of the sour taste of sick. What was going on? She'd drunk two beers and while the pub food wasn't great, you couldn't go wrong with a vegetable stir-fry. Urgh. She wanted to leave.

Pushing open the fling-back door she sought out Mike. Hopefully he'd give her a lift home. As usual, he had his lens focused on the contestants, filming their every word.

She approached and stood behind him waiting, not wanting to interrupt an intimate moment and good viewing. But Zac noticed her lingering and poked his head around Clare and past Mike.

'Tori?' he questioned. 'Are you okay? You're pale.'

'Yeah, I do feel a bit off. Can Mike drive me back to the farm?'

Zac stood and the stool scraped. 'I'll take you. Clare, would you like to stay or call it a night?'

Clare didn't respond to Zac but turned full circle and faced Tori, smirking and raising an eyebrow in question while her eyes twinkled.

'Don't be silly. You cannot call your date short because of me. I'm sure Mike will take me,' Tori stammered.

'I can't leave. I do the filming, Tori.' His words dripped in sarcasm.

Given there wasn't a cab rank of taxis waiting outside to take her home, she had to accept the offer.

Clare stood. 'It's fine. Let's get Tori home if she's not feeling well.'

Zac patted Clare's arm and smiled in her direction while Clare glared at Tori with what looked like smug satisfaction.

What a disaster.

13

The wind picked up and mini tornadoes of dust swirled across the landscape. The branches of the bottle brush trees surrounding Coleman Cattle Station swayed in rhythm and stray leaves rustled along the ground. The breeze cooled the sweat on Zac's skin but he ripped off his hat and wiped the sweat from his brow.

Three station cattle dogs lay on their bellies under the nearest tree, their heads alert, tongues lolling, not prepared to miss any of the action. They rolled around in the dirt to generate some cool. Zac snapped them on his phone and posted to his feed.

#cattledogs #workingdogs #mustering #coolspot

It sure was stinking hot. Too hot to be mustering cattle, but here they all were.

A hard slap landed on his back and that could only mean one thing. Turning, his anticipation built. 'G'day, Chief, you're back!' The men hugged.

'Good to see you, son. You've got a fantastic turn out today.' Mike shoved the camera in their face capturing the greeting.

Chief placed his hand to the lens. 'What's this then?' The man's smile disappeared.

'You've been away too long. I've gotten myself roped into a reality dating show. No guess whose idea it was?' Zac smirked but continued. 'Unfortunately for the time being you'll have to get used to Mike here being a right pain in the behind as he shoves that camera in our faces all the time. You get used to it.'

Chief shook his head but pulled his hand back. 'Mike, I'm Chief.' The two men fumbled to shake hands. 'Zac might have been convinced to find love on TV but give us a break and catch some real action later when the mustering starts.'

Zac nodded at Mike who he assumed had captured the footage he wanted anyway. Mike lowered the camera and wandered away.

'How's the clinic? Have you been busy?'

Zac gave his boss the rundown on births, deaths and emergencies, adding in a few funny stories for good measure. Mid-sentence he paused as his father joined them, talking over him.

'You're a sight Chief. It's great to have you back. Now my son can return to his proper focus here on the station and forget any silliness of working full-time as a vet.'

Zac's mood dipped.

The trio stood under the shade of the tree. Other men participating in the muster gathered in the circular drive, adjacent to the front sheds. Tori busied herself a few metres away, filling an esky with water and snacks for the trip. Tiffany wasn't anywhere.

'Jerome,' Chief nodded at Zac's father. 'You know I'm set for retirement at the end of the year. The valley needs Zac. Without him there's a chance the vet clinic will close and emergencies will have to be handled by the next town. It's too far away and not good for *Cedar Creek Plains*. And, Zac is keen.'

'Zac is keen to do everything possible to avoid his responsibilities here. I'm winding down for retirement too but that doesn't feature in Zac's plans. This is a profitable stud. The best around. I've slaved for years to make it what it is, you can see what I've achieved.' His father waved his hands wide taking in the magnificent homestead.

Chief knew the drill. 'Perhaps it's time to consider a different succession plan Jerome. Accept the boy isn't interested.'

'Perhaps it's time he remembered his responsibility and to do what is required. He'll break his mother's heart if he continues to carry on this way.'

A break-out cat call and whistles came from the group of men to their left. Most were smoking or getting in their last drink before the dusty job ahead.

Zac's shoulders slumped with relief. He unclenched his jaw and rolled out the fists he held at his side and turned. First, he glanced towards Tori and their eyes connected. She stood at the steps to the house, the now filled esky in front of her. Her expression was grim and he guessed she'd overheard the conversation with his father.

Like an oasis in a dry desert, Zac was transfixed by her. Today she wore her trade-mark blue jeans and a cool, light green cotton blouse. Her hair was pulled back in a low ponytail so it draped around her neck. Nothing about what she wore was special but his thirst for her was unquenchable.

He was seriously in trouble.

The noise grew more raucous close by, but Zac's attention was captured by a colourful floating butterfly soaring on the breeze. He wanted to capture it mid-flight but it floated away too fast.

Tiffany had arrived.

She was as colourful as the butterfly. Zac had suspected

Tiffany was no wallflower and today proved it. She lapped up the attention from the male group, held one hand to her hip and stood in that funny way girls do, with one leg bent out and her hip angled to the side.

Normal blue-rinse jeans were accompanied by a black top but the reflection off the large gold buckle belt she wore had him squinting before he could register the bubble-gum pink knee-high boots. The colour paled in comparison to the bouffant blonde blow wave she wore. Very American.

With the crowd watching on, she sauntered over to him, placed one hand behind his head and pulled him in for a smooch on the lips. The kiss drew jeers from the men and cheers for more.

His father muttered behind him to Chief. 'And that's the other thing the boy got himself involved in. A stupid dating show. I don't know how it happened but his priorities are all screwed.'

The roars drowned out his father's voice. Zac's chest tightened and his face grew hot. Averting his gaze, he observed the red dirt on the ground and how it covered his boots but had not yet coloured Tiffany's. Glancing back up, a salacious grin greeted him and a dozen gazes burned into him, heavy and expectant. Sweat gathered on his brow, he twisted the pinkie ring with his thumb and turned his gaze to Tori who held up a bottle of water, gesturing for him to approach.

Zac nodded and grasped Tiffany's hand and headed toward the homestead. Mike filmed and Zac understood it would make terrible television. This was the moment he was supposed to dip his date and kiss her passionately to the cries of the local blokes and the women watching at home. He knew how he was supposed to act; but the only thing on his mind was escape and Tori offered it.

'Thank you,' he whispered as he clutched the icy cold bottle of water. Tiffany resisted but he dragged her along until they were inside the house and the door shut. Inside he dropped her hand and rolled the water bottle over his hot face.

14

———

'Anyone checked out Zac's feed today? He posted the dogs. They're so cute,' cooed Lara.

Zac's four sisters gathered around the one phone to check out the image.

'Have you seen Zac's Instagram account, Tori? It's adorable. It's all animal photos in a whole range of different shots. You won't see any family or social pics. A bit weird but super-fun.'

Tori moved closer and agreed it was a great photo and made a mental note to check it out later.

'It's so fabulous to have you back. Are you staying?' asked Eliza, Zac's eldest sister.

Tori sat at the grand outdoor table that covered the entire width of the verandah wrapping around the Coleman homestead. Today it was decked out with an excessive amount of food for lunch when she wasn't even hungry.

'You know what? I think I might.' The women cheered.

'Another eligible woman to add to the few available. If we'd known, we might not have volunteered baby brother for the show.' Lara, the youngest sister, peeked at Tori with an expression she couldn't interpret.

'I heard you signed him up. Bet he was pleased?'

'He knew when he was defeated and he'd never live it down if he didn't proceed. No was not an option. He's a smart guy; understood when to give in,' said Hollie, the second youngest and one of the duo of sisters that had written Zac's application for the show.

'I know I've been gone a long time, but why did you need to? All the girls drooled over him at school. He was voted most boyfriend-worthy and he was dating Susie,' Tori said.

'Oh, so long ago,' Eliza crooned. 'Susie, I remember her. Wild curly hair like Nicole Kidman and very sweet.'

Jessica nursed a sleeping baby of about six-months and rocked the bundle as she spoke. 'His confidence was knocked by the cancer scare a few years back and he hasn't dated much since. He needs a bit of a boost and we thought being chased by four women at once might do the trick. But we also secretly hope he might find love. He deserves to be happy.'

Each sister nodded.

'Who do you think is the front runner?' Tori asked, the question causing a bunch of little firecrackers to release in her tummy.

'Well, not Tiffany given his reaction this morning. And she was dressed like a grown-up lollypop in that outfit. Zac is so not going to go for that,' offered Hollie.

'Sophie is gorgeous,' said Tori and waited for their reactions.

'And she's a teacher which is fabulous,' said Lara, her sisters booing in response.

'Only because you're a teacher. Doesn't mean she's perfect for Zac. I think he'll be too intimidated by her perfection and elegance,' said Jessica. 'I think it's either the osteopath, Lucy, because she's so sensible or the country girl, Clare.'

'Clare gives off a funny vibe, don't you think?' commented Eliza.

There were a few murmurs of agreement.

'No matter who he chooses, let's hope he gives up that ridiculous notion of not wanting children. I mean, it's crazy. He comes from a large family, has adorable nieces and nephews whom he loves but says he doesn't want children.' Jessica held up her own bub and kissed its forehead as if justifying her argument.

'He doesn't want children?' Tori squeaked the words.

'Tori, he claims he doesn't, but none of us believe him,' exclaimed Eliza.

Hollie held her head in her hands, 'Imagine if he's told any of the women that view.'

'He can't have. They'd have run, wouldn't they? Most women want children. Tori, you do. How old is your daughter?' asked Eliza.

'Mirry is four.' She had difficulty forming the words. All of a sudden, Tori's body overheated. She gulped down a glass of water and fanned out her shirt. The sisters kept nattering on oblivious.

Zac didn't want children.

The guy had kissed her! How dare he? She had a daughter, he'd saved her bloody guinea pigs from near death after all, had tendered to them with so much love.

Tori recalled the few occasions Mirry and Zac had been together. He'd doted on her or had she imagined it? The sister's voices receded as she tried to remember. No, he *had* doted on her. They'd played together and Zac had giggled and even made faces. Mirry had found it hilarious. Something Todd had never done, come down to her level and played with her like she was important and special.

The man who tended with such care to injured animals; gave them his one hundred percent, didn't want children.

Then he couldn't possibly want her.

The realisation hit her hard.

Had she really thought Zac wanted her?

The pesky nausea that had been bothering her for days surfaced again. Maybe it was the prawns but she couldn't keep making excuses.

The sour and acidic taste entered her mouth. Tori breathed deeply in and out to make the sensation go away and to calm her racing heart. Her entire body shook with the effort. But she couldn't do it; couldn't hold it together and she raced for the railing and vomited over the edge.

Each sister rushed towards her; one patting her back, the other holding her hair, another offering a cup of water.

She'd grown up with these girls so they were like sisters. The homestead had been her playground for horse riding, bonfires and annual festivals. And now they cared for her. Who wouldn't want this for themselves? A loving family to surround yourself with; to care for you, nurture you and love you. It didn't make any sense. As an only child it was often all she'd dreamed about having when she grew up. And to be a better mother than the one she'd had.

Tori's eyes watered as her entire lunch ended up in the front garden.

15

————

Two pink lines.

No! No! No! Tori screamed a silent scream, covered her gaping mouth and glanced around in case someone saw, in case someone witnessed her fear. She'd been blindsided. It could be wrong. It was common for false positives, right? She'd do another test.

She did the test again.

Same result.

Tori lay curled up into a ball on her side, a bed on the enclosed back verandah offering a welcome retreat. Her finger swiped over the screen of her phone.

How cute could one man be? Despite her predicament, which she was blissfully ignoring for a few minutes, she scrolled through Zac's Instagram. An entire feed of animal photos with most of them capturing large doses of cuteness.

Tears pricked her eyes at the images. The account was so adorable that she couldn't understand how Zac wouldn't want to fill a similar feed with photographs of gorgeous little babies.

The idea of him not wanting to was so far out of the ballpark of anything she might imagine about Zac. Zac who was perfect in almost every way.

Instead, she focused on the baby kittens curled beside their mother not long after being born, and the sheep under a burning horizon sun and the many dogs of all breeds and poses. Puddles and Rainbow! She paused her quick finger scroll. When did he capture those two rascals? Tori spread her fingers wide and zoomed into the background. Nan's house. Must have been when he returned them or perhaps when they escaped. A line of animal emojis featured as his comment.

His sisters were right. Not a single photo of anything else, no previous flames or drunken Saturday night shots at the pub. All animals in their glorious rural outback.

Her stomach cramped again and she curled up tighter.

Tori placed one hand on her belly. A little life grew in there. She didn't feel nauseous anymore but wretched in every definition of the word. And oh, so tired. Right at this moment she wanted to lay on this bed for a week and not move; let the world continue around her.

She wished. Reality had hit her smack in the face and she had to rise to the challenge.

And she would, but, oh, how could she have been so stupid? Dumb enough to get pregnant again to her loser of a husband who preferred sex with other women.

But even worse how could she not have realised? She knew the signs for goodness sake; had been pregnant before. In fairness she'd been distracted recently. Yes, with leaving that same unfaithful husband, caring for her daughter and relocating themselves to the country where she hoped to develop a thriving business. Not to mention Zac.

After vomiting, the sisters had ushered her inside to clean up and rest. In the bathroom at the rear of the house, she'd washed her face and tidied her hair, and searched for some light make-up to hide the circles under her eyes and make her lips shine again.

She didn't mean to snoop. But as soon as she saw the pregnancy kit hidden amongst the bottles and tubes, she'd realised. She'd fallen back onto her bottom on the cold tiled floor and pieced together the obvious signs over the last couple of weeks.

It wasn't like her to steal someone else's stuff, but she'd been unable to resist. Tori had to know for sure. Right then.

Yep, she was pregnant.

Tori flicked off the phone and pushed her face into the pillow and cried. She'd never felt so alone.

TORI ROUSED TO RAISED VOICES OUTSIDE THE WINDOW. STRETCHING out her legs it took a few moments before realisation kicked in and the world crashed back down around her.

Instinctively she patted her stomach again before raising up onto an elbow and peering out the window. The sun was less ferocious and a shadow had commenced to creep across the back yard. The manicured lawn and garden beds blossomed with reds, pinks and yellow. Tori had to admit, the vista was pretty idyllic. There was something about dry sprawling plains creeping up to meet vibrant green grass with the explosions of colour.

To her left Tiffany came into view. She was nothing like the woman who had left mustering this morning, not a sign of the gusto and confidence she'd displayed as she'd kissed Zac.

This woman dragged her no longer pristine boots against the ground as she walked with a slight limp. The magnificent bouffant curls were flat and hung lifeless around her shoulders, an Akubra hat hanging from her hand. The left leg of her jeans was smattered with brown patches that also crawled up her shirt sleeve. When she turned in Tori's direction, both cheeks were caked in sticky wet mud with little bits flaking away as she walked.

But it was her scowl that had Tori stifling a giggle.

Pinching her own cheeks to add colour to what she was sure must have been a pale complexion, Tori wandered out and through the homestead.

Jessica held an awake baby now and stood watching the show on the deck as it unfurled in front of her. Both Hollie and Lara were fussing over Tiffany who swatted their hands away.

For once Tori wished Mike was here to capture the footage. This is exactly what the viewers wanted, didn't they?

'What's happened?' Tori asked.

'Apparently, she was attacked by a stud - her words - and had to run for her life but no one came to her assistance,' Jessica's eyebrows were raised, her eyes twinkling.

'So she's come back early and alone?' Tori searched for Zac.

'Yup.'

'How on earth did she find her way?'

'She was mounted on Rufus. That old girl would find her way back to the homestead through a blizzard. So lucky for Tiffany she would have led her right home,' Jessica offered.

Hollie and Lara attempted to placate an enraged Tiffany with kind words, wet towels and a cold drink. Tiffany rejected the offers and stormed off to the sheds.

'It won't be too long until the group is back,' Jessica said, 'We're hanging out in the kitchen. Come and join us.'

Tori nodded and followed.

'Are you feeling better?'

16

Zac pulled open the heavy oak doors to the barn and all he could think about was quenching his thirst with an ice-cold beer.

The lads surrounding him jostled for a spot to cool down their horses or park their motorbikes as quickly as possible to allow the celebrations to begin.

His eyes adjusted to the dimness of indoors and he spotted two figures in one of the bays; Zac pulled up sharp. A couple of musterers bumped into his back before going quiet and then all six of them exploded into raucous guffaws and wolf whistles, their profanities loud and unruly.

Tiffany gasped. She twisted around towards the commotion, her bright blue eyes wide like her gaping mouth.

In front of her stood a young rouse-about employed by Zac's father. His lips were in a smooched position, one hand clasped to Tiffany's waist, the other clearly inside her top, enjoying the curves of her voluptuous bust.

Tiffany's mouth closed and with alacrity she extracted his hand and slapped the young guy hard across the cheek.

Mike arrived on the scene. Skidding on his feet in the dirt and fumbling to get his camera rolling. Zac had seen him over by the entry stairs, looking exhausted when he'd briefly put his camera down for a rest.

Tiffany didn't acknowledge the gathering crowd. Instead she turned and stormed off through the rear door of the barn. Mike swung the camera in Zac's face to catch his reaction before swinging back away and chasing after Tiffany.

A few men approached the jackaroo and slapped him on the back, congratulating him on the conquest. Zac approached and stood in front of him and the group hushed, aware the young man, whose name no one knew, had been making out with one of Zac's contestants.

The man flinched as Zac reached up and whacked him on the back too. 'Looks like you saved me a whole lot of trouble. Thanks mate.'

The men cheered.

It didn't take long for word to travel. By the time Zac had cleaned up and changed clothes, Anna Fox was at the station. Mike stood by her side while the crowd sat on hay bales shadowed by flickering fairy lights hanging from the trees.

Zac's heart sat heavy in his chest as he took in the scene.

His four sisters stood to the side and Eliza moved forward in step with him. She grasped his arm in solidarity but dropped it as he moved away towards Anna. Tori stood further back, closer to the verandah and his whole body came alive with longing.

He had almost reached Anna when from his right a figure

barrelled towards him in a flurry of colour and floating on a cloud of strong perfume. A flat palm was to his cheek before he could blink.

'Bastard. You should have rescued me from that cow. It could have killed me!' Tiffany's face was scrunched in fury before she circled and stormed off.

'Well, there you have it folks,' Anna crooned into the camera, 'love doesn't always run smoothly. Tiffany has decided farmer Zac and rural life isn't for her and is the first girl to leave the show. Three remain, which one will Zac choose?'

Mike filmed a panorama of the celebrations in front of him and then followed Tiffany's departing back.

'Zac, we want you to give us a round-up of how you feel about Tiffany leaving. Okay?' Anna prompted when he didn't respond.

'Okay,' he said and reached for the beer he'd been dreaming of.

Anna approached Tori and with their heads bent, Anna whispered something to her. Tori nodded and glanced in his direction but her expression was blank.

Victoria.

The wind rustled her loose dark hair and her skin dazzled in the afternoon haze. All of the commotion around him receded, forgotten.

She was the one that brightened his spirits. Her presence that made his heart skip a beat and was always the only one he wanted to talk to. It was Tori who mattered. Always had been. He'd known it but had gone along with this ridiculous façade. A cracking pain shot across his chest, physical confirmation of the disaster he'd created. What the hell was he going to do? At the moment he couldn't be with her.

But that was all he wanted.

Victoria stared right through him. Her mouth was down-turned and her eyes hooded. Sad. Lost. Like an invisible pull of gravity he moved towards her. If she was in pain, he wanted to help. Needed to help.

But the next time he looked up, Tori was gone.

'Mummy!' Mirry cried and rushed towards her car as it pulled to a park outside of Nan's place. 'Daddy's here!'

Tori's head jerked up so fast it cracked. Sure enough, short blonde curls on a lean frame sauntered out of the shadows and into the glare of the afternoon sun. 'What the fuck?' she muttered as she unclipped her seat belt and opened the door, her movements in slow motion to allow her to regulate her breaths and calm the hell down.

The little girl jumped up and down on the spot. Tori leaned down to her height and squeezed her in close for a cuddle. Something hard jabbed at her belly and pinched. Tori pulled back and Mirry squealed again and held up three new Barbie dolls. Two wore active wear and the third some ridiculous pale lemon ball gown. For some reason the active wear bristled. Old life and sore memories perhaps?

So, Todd was going to be one of those dads, prepared to pull out all the tricks in the war for Mirry's affection.

He approached and stood before her. 'Hi.'

'You could have told me you were coming to visit.'

'Would you have let me?'

She scoffed. 'Of course. You can visit Mirry anytime. You are her father, after all.'

'I wanted to see you, too.'

Tori stared incredulous. 'What for? To tell me all about your new love pad? Shacked up together now, have you?'

Todd moved in closer and clasped her elbow. There was slight yet familiar body odour, tangy and acidic; like he'd been working out. He leaned too close. She'd forgotten how strong his grip was.

'I'm sorry. It didn't mean anything. I love you.'

Tori ripped her arm away. His touch repulsed her.

'It meant something when you were going for it up against the wall. You weren't even hiding. So desperate to get into each other's pants were you?' Tori lashed out at him.

'Daddy, c'mon. I'll show you 'round. There are so many animals. Do you want to say hi to Puddles and Rainbow? They almost died!' Mirry tugged her father's hand but his eyes remained fixed on Tori, pleading. Their connection broke as Mirry pulled him away to see the farm.

'Urgh!' She slammed the car door shut too hard and stormed inside.

Nan found her kneading the dough for the fresh bread she planned to serve with dinner. Her stomach churned, a mixture of nausea and anger.

'Go easy or the bread will never rise.' Nan patted her on the arm.

'Who does he think he is, Nan? Coming here, turning up whenever he chooses.'

'He hasn't seen Mirabelle for over two weeks. She's delighted to see him.'

'He can see Mirry and she deserves to spend time with her father. It's not that. He can't turn up whenever he likes.'

Nan smiled, her wise green eyes crinkling.

'God, I can't even put into words what I'd like to do to him. That image of him, him, *fucking that woman*,' Tori whispered the phrase, 'is back bouncing around in my head. I'm not like my mother, weak and forgiving, a dreamer.'

Nan interrupted her again. 'Your mother was not weak. In fact, she was the opposite: strong and headfast and determined. You have all those qualities too and they are not bad traits.'

'I don't want those qualities if it means you leave behind your responsibilities to chase bigger and better opportunities. Opportunities you couldn't have with a little girl in tow. I understand more now I'm a mother. I could never, ever, leave Mirry, not ever.' Tori paused her overzealous mixing and blew her fringe out of her eyes.

She kept on. 'I can't believe you still defend her after all these years. She's cut both of us out of her life and yet you speak fondly of her.'

'If Mirry abandoned you, regardless of the circumstances, you'd still love her too. Doesn't mean you love her behaviour or the way she's treated you, but she's my daughter. And the best thing she ever did was leave you with me. I adored having you around when you were growing up. Kept me young again.'

Tori wiped her flour-covered hands on her apron while tears rolled down her cheeks and they held each other tight.

'I did the same too, anyway. I shouldn't criticise. I left you, too.'

'Ah, that was more spreading your wings, I think. Discovering who you were. And look at you now, a mother, business owner and fabulous cook!'

'Hardly, but said like a true loving grandmother. Sorry, Nan. But I know one thing I am not and that is a pushover. Some people are prepared to give philandering husbands another go, I'm not. If he didn't want to remain married to me and wanted to be with whatever her name is, he could have gone about it the right way. He didn't. I could never trust him again. And thanks to him, I may never trust a man again.'

'Okay, so you treat this as a father visiting his daughter. He can stay for dinner. For longer if he makes arrangements to stay.' Tori went to butt in but Nan held up her palm. 'I didn't say here. We're fully booked anyway. Give him some time to work it out.'

Wiping her moist cheeks, she nodded. 'You're right. And I have a dinner to prepare.' She kissed her nan's cheek and went back to her happy place.

17

Tori was deliberately being a bitch. But damnit, she couldn't help it.

Sure enough Todd was hanging around and joining them for dinner. Well, eating with Mirry, as Tori wouldn't be sitting down nice and cosy with *her husband*. She had to work anyway and prepare the dinner for the show tonight. Plus, she had to get away from Todd's puppy dogs eyes that followed her every move.

Because of their special guest, she took extra care with the meal. Todd had converted her to veganism but she wasn't strict compared to him. He was hard-core about the food he ate. So, she'd cooked a good old-fashioned roast beef with all the trimmings, including gravy with animal fats and vegetables soaked in dripping. The bread was vegan but she'd keep that to herself. Dessert was cheesecake because Todd loved his gelatine…

Tori gripped her belly as a wave of nausea washed over her. That would teach her for being evil. But still, she couldn't wait to see the look on his face as dinner was served. Would he make a fuss or enjoy dinner with his daughter? This wasn't an *a la carte* restaurant; there was no sending your dinner back.

Todd positioned himself at the high benches in the kitchen in readiness to eat with her and Nan. Nice try. Tori directed him to a special table for two in the alcove where the other B&B guests would dine while the television show was filmed in the main room.

'This is romantic,' Todd said as his eyes sparkled in her direction.

Tori clasped Mirry's hand and guided her to the table. 'Yes,' Tori smirked, 'a special daddy and daughter dinner.' Todd didn't even mimic a smile. But Mirry felt special.

The main room hummed with activity as the remaining three contestants and Zac dined with Anna, Mike trawling the room as usual.

'Where's Tiffany?' asked Clare.

Anna stood at the head of the table and advised Tiffany had left the show that afternoon. Mike's camera scanned their faces for reactions. Anna's words took a few moments to sink in and the reactions varied – relief at less competition, to sorrow (such a terrible way to go) and pure nasty happiness. It took less than a refill of their drinks for the women to forget about poor Tiffany. Their focus intensified on Zac; he was prey in their sights.

'Zac,' Lucy sidled up to him and clutched his arm. Her preferred casual workout gear and flat shoes – heels are so bad for your back – were nowhere in sight. Tonight she wore a little black number that showed off her shapely legs and accentuated her red hair. 'Let's go outside for a chat while we wait for dinner.'

Zac gazed back at her like a deer stunned in headlights. 'I'll bring you both out a drink,' Tori jumped in, feeling uncomfortable on his behalf. Nice one Lucy. A Bachelorette type move. Would it pay off?

Tori delivered the drinks, but clearly she didn't work as fast as Lucy. They stood in the far corner of the verandah with Zac's back to the balustrade appearing as if he was trapped.

Tori lingered out of sight behind the open French doors while her fingers frosted around the cold drinks.

She couldn't see what Lucy was doing but she imagined the woman's hands pawing at Zac's chest, her fingers twirling through the smattering of hair escaping the top of his shirt.

'Zac, I've enjoyed your company. I know it's not just me. You know we have a fantastic future together. It can work for us. My business is transportable and perfect for the country.' Did she purr? Lucy stepped closer to him, any closer and she'd be straddling him. 'I'm falling for you,' her voice was low and husky.

Tori growled low in her throat. Her gaze lowered to the golden Aperol Spritz she held. It would go nicely down the front of Lucy's dazzling black dress. Okay, she wouldn't. Imagine that being caught on film? The viewers would love the twist. A crew member goes off script the headline might say.

No, she wouldn't toss the drink at Lucy, but she damn well couldn't stand still either. Her feet moved and she clomped out the door. Zac flinched and tried to move away but Lucy was attached to his face.

Grow some balls Zac, she wanted to scream. Hurt someone's feelings for a change. Instead, she said in a high-pitched voice, 'Here are your lovely cool drinks. It's warm out here tonight.' She stood behind them as Lucy stepped back from Zac but didn't turn. Zac accepted the drinks and handed one to her.

'Dinner won't be long,' she said in her sing-song voice.

'Thank you, Victoria.'

'Yes, thank you Tori. You're always around at the most

convenient times,' Lucy said as she swirled around and offered a saccharine smile. Her body jerked on the turn and she tugged at one leg in an unladylike fashion. The orange liquid spilt over the lip of the glass and dripped down her leg. 'Argh,' Lucy said. Her stiletto was caught in the gap of the old timber floorboards.

Leaning over and showing off too much butt, she yanked at the shoe that wouldn't budge. Removing her foot from the stranded shoe, she stood lopsided.

'These were new and expensive. Now one is stuck in your deck,' Lucy said to Tori.

'I'm awfully sorry. I'll find something to wrench it out with.'

Lucy skulled the remnants of her drink and handed the empty glass to Tori before smiling through tight lips and hobbling away unevenly.

Tori scampered away, too, to avoid Zac. She didn't want to look at him and know what he was thinking. Didn't want to communicate about what had happened and how she'd acted in successfully sabotaging their intimate moment. She should feel ecstatic, but her belly churned.

As she moved away she observed the full and bright white moon illuminating the sky, twinkling stars surrounding it. Ah well, the romantic setting hadn't worked.

18

———

Tori stepped into the bright lights of the dining room. Mike and Sophie moved swiftly apart and Sophie wiped one finger along the corner of her lips. Mike rose from the seat at the table, his belt buckle loose.

What was that? Mike and well, anyone, but Sophie? The most elegant lady in the group groping the cameraman, who in Tori's view was a lazy misogynist. Geez, what was Sophie doing?

With wide eyes and unable to hide her surprise, Tori turned back to Zac as he followed behind her. Lucky, his head was lowered so he hadn't seen anything.

Even Clare was glassy-eyed and sat slouched in her chair with one arm slung over the back. The number of empty glasses on the table in front of her, the answer.

The night sure was taking an interesting turn.

Zac sat and Tori scooted off to serve dinner. Some food in rumbling tummies might ensure everyone behaved themselves. Even her?

Nan had served the other guests whilst she was interrupting Zac and Lucy so Tori delivered the main meals to the *Local Lads Looking for Love* crew and contestants. The group concentrated on their meals but tension filled the air.

She stepped into the alcove. 'Well done with your dinner, sweetheart. Did you like it?' she asked Mirry taking in Todd's uneaten plate. He'd nibbled at a few of the vegetables. The slab of meat remained untouched, its bulk congealed in gravy soup. The bread was gone.

'Yummy, thank you Mummy,' Mirry said as she yawned.

'Time for bed, kiddo. Kiss Daddy good night and head upstairs. Nan will come and see you soon.' The little girl rose on skinny legs and hugged her father.

The moment Mirry left the room, Todd clutched her arm, the grip too tight. 'We need to talk.'

'Stop grabbing me like you never intend to let me go.' Tori pulled her arm back and her glasses slid down her nose. She pushed them back up with too much force. 'You have no right to touch me.'

Surprisingly, Todd let go. Her tone was harsh, she guessed, and she'd rarely spoken to him like that before.

Tori left him and entered the main dining room.

'I love you,' Todd yelled and the room fell silent.

Tori paused mid-step and hoped by some miracle the ground would open up and swallow her. Instead, Todd chased her. He stood so close behind she heard his intake of breath before he kept speaking.

'I'm sorry for what I've done.'

Tori did not want to turn; did not want to acknowledge him. But all eyes in the room burned into her.

She glanced around in slow motion. Todd was on one knee and holding up a blue jewellery box.

'Let's start again.'

Mike moved to her left, focusing the camera on her and Todd. Tori shook her head towards the camera but Mike either didn't see or choose to ignore her plea. He would do pretty much anything to capture good footage, so it was probably the latter.

'I love you, Victoria Christensen. I made a mistake. Please forgive me?'

'What did he do?' Clare sang out.

'Slept with the Pilates instructor at their gym,' Mike responded.

What the? That man had eyes and ears everywhere. Important to remember.

'Bastard,' both Clare and Sophie echoed.

At that moment Tori liked them very much.

Todd shoved the box into her hands and Tori pushed it back, but Todd kept ramming it into her palm.

Embarrassment pulsed through her and Tori glanced at Zac. He'd know what to do, how she should react. Her childhood friend had always been a calming influence. His eyes were wide and they were streaked with sympathy. No, she'd wanted to draw strength from him. But his concern almost undid her and the tight control she was holding onto. Suddenly she was tired. Tired of fighting, working so hard to always be the good girl, to be the best wife and parent, always being responsible.

Zac gathered himself and rose and stood next to her; he didn't speak or touch her, knowing his presence was what she needed. That she could look after herself, that even though she might need it, she didn't want to be saved. It was an act of solidarity that she loved and it spurred her on.

Loud, ugly sobs rose out of Todd that caused his face to turn a blotchy red and scrunch up in an unattractive way.

Of course it wasn't the right time or place. Oh, well, he started it.

'The answer is no. You ruined our marriage and our family by sleeping with someone else. You made a mistake and I no longer trust you nor love you.' Tori placed the blue box on the ground in front of him. He picked it up and threw it at her. Zac reached across her to catch it but he missed and it fell onto the rug. Sophie jumped out of her chair.

'That is no way to treat jewellery. It deserves respect.'

Tori's head went heavy on her shoulders and she swayed. A kaleidoscope of colour flickered behind her eyelids. She reached for the dining chair for support and Zac placed his hand to her back.

'I'm pregnant!' Her voice was too loud and out of control. *You stupid idiotic fuck*, she wanted to scream. 'While you were busy screwing someone else, I was carrying your child and looking after Mirry.' She held back her tears, did not want to be weak.

'Who's the dad?' Mike asked, his head popping out to the left of camera. 'I mean you are separated and all.'

'Are you for real?' she replied with venom.

'Yeah, who's the father? How do I know it's me?' Todd joined in.

Tori's fury dissolved like a deflating balloon. All of the oxygen left the room as she tried to think of a riposte.

'You're a terrible husband. I hope you're a better father to our children.'

She'd moved beyond anger to not caring anymore. It was an unusual sensation. It created a sense of power and control she relished. Todd was a waste of her time. She left the room and clicked the kitchen door shut behind her. The dining room erupted in a cacophony of noise as people spoke over each other. Mike would be loving this, Anna too, or perhaps not, because the drama didn't relate to the show.

Tori stood leaning back against the door listening as if she was someone else.

19

Zac downed the last of his beer. What a crap night. Good television viewing? He wasn't sure. Did people want to watch all that drama?

Luckily the segment with Lucy wasn't captured. It was embarrassing. For both of them. Thank goodness Victoria had arrived in time.

A baby goat wandered past the front stairs where he sat. Its white fur illuminated in the verandah light. It paused and stared at him with glowing eyes. One go and he had the perfect picture. It was a beauty. The tiny goat was outlined by the bright moon high in the sky but was contrasted with the deep green of the grass it stood upon, its captivating gaze staring down the lens. It gave him a lift. He loved capturing creatures in their natural environment.

#goatlove #kids #farmlife

The door creaked open.

He knew it was her without looking.

'I'm sorry about that rat of a husband of yours,' he said as Tori sat next to him on the top step.

'I'm sorry that scene ruined the evening and probably the show.'

Zac shrugged. 'It was all a bit of a disaster. But is it congratulations about the baby?'

Victoria shrugged now. 'Yes, and no. The circumstances suck. A poor baby being welcomed into a fractured family with a less than perfect father. But it is what it is, I guess. I'll love it regardless and do my best to be a good mother.'

'So, it's one lucky baby indeed.'

Victoria lightly shoved her shoulder against his in thanks. 'Only the cocktail party left. Do you know what you're going to do?'

'No.' He answered. 'I honestly don't.'

'I still don't get it. You say you didn't want to be on the show but here you are. It's all been, well, mundane from what I've seen. The dates haven't been great, is that fair to say? I don't understand why you bothered. These girls have feelings and real lives. They may have entered the show hoping to find love.'

'I did too, after the initial shock and anger. I agreed because I thought maybe, I might meet a nice girl.'

'A nice girl?' Victoria challenged him. 'Zac, you are the most eligible bachelor in town. All of the girls lust after you and the women on the show would match up with you in a heartbeat. It doesn't make any sense.'

'I've fought them off over the years.' Victoria laughed and held her stomach. He loved the sound. 'Sorry, I don't mean there's been hundreds of women beating down my door. I mean there's been a few, but, I don't know. It was never right.'

'But don't you want a relationship? Have a family? Settle down? Be loved?'

He turned sideways to face her. 'I want all of those things.' His words were forceful. 'But I can't.'

'Of course you can. You have a loving family, a job, dreams, a life. Lots of women would fall for you. Plus, you're the nicest bloke I know.'

He paused. Maybe it was time to be honest with Victoria. 'You know how I told you I had cancer?'

She nodded, watching, waiting for him to continue.

'The treatment left me sterile. I'm unable to have children.' He let the revelation sink in. 'It's unfair to ask a woman to accept that. I know the value of family, I grew up with lots of siblings. I don't want to be responsible for robbing someone of their dreams. So, I'm not a great package, regardless of the rest. I made a decision a long time ago that I'd be fine by myself. I love my nieces and nephews and my animals. I can have a full and happy life.'

'But it isn't that simple, is it?' Victoria reached over and held his hand in hers. It was warm and soft. 'I'm so sorry you had to go through that experience. But you know what? The power of love is incredible. If someone loves you for who you are, they are enormously forgiving. Particularly of flaws, not that I'm saying it's a flaw. More of an obstacle. And plus, this is the twenty-first century. There are so many options.'

'Clare told me she doesn't want children and it wasn't negotiable. Said it was important I knew.'

'Did you tell her?'

'No. I've never told anyone.'

'What? You haven't told your family you can't have children and that is the reason you've remained single all these years?'

Zac nodded.

'Man, that's crazy. Zac, they love you. And would regardless.

Perhaps it might have kept your sisters off your back about getting married.'

'I've been living in the shadow of my family forever. They're so suffocating and noisy and demanding. They think they have a right to know everything. I guess it's one reason I've kept it back. My way of keeping some control.'

'Your dad is one tough cookie.'

'You think? Dad interferes in my work and my sisters interfere in my personal life. All bases are covered.'

'They love you though. It sounds like a dream to someone who has no family. That's why I'll welcome this baby because I never had a family and I want one.'

Zac slapped his knee and the sound reverberated through the dark and still night. 'Exactly my point.'

'Maybe it's time nice-guy Zac stood up for himself? It doesn't mean people won't like you. People will admire you for chasing your dreams, for sticking up for yourself. It's time.'

'When did life become so complicated?'

'When we grew up, I guess.'

Victoria placed her arms around his middle and held him close. His breath caught. This was the reaction he searched for with each of the contestants. With her it felt good, and right and he always wanted her close.

'What will you do now?' he asked her as he inhaled the vanilla and raspberry scent of her hair.

'Work out how to be alone.'

'So, no forgiving Todd?'

'No, I'm certain. But otherwise, I'm thinking of staying. I've missed out on so much time with Nan. She never sees her daughter, my mum, and she's here all alone. I know she's fine. But I want to spend time with her and I love this lifestyle for

Mirry. She adores the animals and learning to care for them; horse riding and running around barefoot each afternoon.'

Zac tried not to move. It was hard when butterflies were going crazy in his belly and he wanted to dance with joy. Plain and simple, he liked having her around. He put his arms around her shoulders and together they cuddled.

'I think you can achieve anything you want.'

'Why is it that I don't trust men and yet feel comfortable with you Zachary Coleman?'

A faint click in the front yard had them both on alert. Zac felt empty the moment Victoria removed her arms. He wanted them back on him, their bodies touching and skin close.

'What was that?' They both scanned the yard.

'Is that a glow in my car?' Zac sat up taller to gain a better vantage.

'Sure is, maybe the light from a phone screen,' she offered. A person lifted their phone closer to their face and they could see.

'Sophie. She's sitting in your car.'

Zac's body sagged. 'The night is not yet over...'

Victoria got a fit of the giggles. 'Does she think you won't notice her holed up in your car? Hoping you'll drive home and she'll jump out and surprise you? Hope she'll strike it lucky?'

Zac stared at her and held his lips together in a tight line. 'Clearly she doesn't know me well. I'm not that sort of guy. Sometimes I wish I was. I could have a bit of fun and forget about it all tomorrow.'

'But then you wouldn't be Zac anymore. You'd be like every other guy.'

She kissed him on the cheek. It was innocent, but her eyes remained shut and her moist lips lingered; he inched his body closer. Did she savour it as much as he did? All too soon it was over.

20

The next morning after a restless night tossing and turning and thinking about Zac, Tori poured Nan a coffee.

He did want a family.

In the early hours when she couldn't sleep, she'd made decisions, but not about Zac. About her.

Tori handed Nan the mug. 'I love you, Nan,' she said and Nan glanced up from the morning paper.

'I love you, too, honey.'

'I want to stay here with Mirry and the baby. Can I help run the farm and B&B and take some of the load off you a little. I'll be responsible for all of the meals, of course. And I'll continue to try and get my catering business up and running as well. But, well, can we stay?'

Nan's eyes misted over. 'I'd love that so much, Tori. I don't need your help, girl, but I'd like it and your company and to spend precious time with your children.'

Tori hugged her from behind then served up scrambled eggs and generously buttered toast.

'You've made a decision about the type of catering too, then?' Her Nan asked pointing to the dairy injected eggs.

Tori smiled. 'Well, yeah. A less restrictive menu might be more successful. Particularly here in *Cedar Creek Plains* and local areas. Plus, all of a sudden it feels like that life was all about Todd. I remember now about the origins of food and how healthy and delicious home-made can be. You can't go wrong with home-grown and fresh ingredients, right? It's better than nouveau vegan food that excludes a number of food groups. And plus, it's been so much fun making those scrumptious desserts from my childhood.'

'It must be the French in you.' Nan smiled.

'Maybe. But they're so damn yummy too!'

There was a faint knock to the back door and it pushed open to reveal Todd.

Tori placed the spatula she held on the bench and took a breath. 'Morning,' she said.

Taken aback Todd paused and his eyebrows rose in question. 'Morning,' he replied hesitantly. He stood like he waited for the spatula to be thrown at his head. And of course, he deserved that. But after chatting with Zac something had clicked and Tori knew she had to sort out her relationship with her children's father plus her future, and that's exactly what she intended to do; starting now.

'Come in,' she continued. 'Nan, is it okay if Todd and I go for a walk? I think it's time we chatted about the future and the arrangements for him to see Mirry and the bub when it arrives.' Tori patted her belly.

'What? You're staying here?' he spluttered.

'Yes, it's time for a chat,' Nan agreed. 'I'll hold the fort. Off you go,' and she shooed them out of the kitchen.

Tori hugged her grandmother again and squeezed tight.

Nan whispered in her ear. 'Now you need to find a hard-working, reliable and loyal country boy. A man who will love you ferociously.'

'Even if I find him, Nan, how will I ever trust him?'

'Chief, I owe you. I can't ever repay what you've done for me. Thank you, for everything.'

Zac's fingers danced across the paperwork.

Chief slapped him on the back. 'My time away made me realise I'd like to travel more and work less. I've loved this job and this town and the animals, but it's time to stop now. I have an itch to get into the caravan with Joan and travel around Australia, see what else is outside of these plains.'

He continued, 'I'm so happy to know the clinic is in good hands and so is the future of this region with you responsible for the animals. That's the reason I've brought forward my retire-ment. I trust you. You'll do a great job. The time is right.'

Zac choked up. His dream was coming true. He was forging his own future and breaking free from control. He finished his signature with a flourish and hugged the man who'd taught him all he knew and acted more as a father figure than his own.

'Do you want me to come and see your father with you?'

'Nah. You don't want to be part of any fiasco. You'll hear his reaction from here anyway.' Zac grinned, but his insides churned at the showdown about to occur. It wouldn't be pretty.

'Good luck, son. I'll pass this to my lawyer and we'll do a formal handover this week.'

They shook hands and Zac hopped straight into his ute and headed to his folk's place. Best to get the confrontation over with. Checking the time on the dashboard he hoped he'd catch his parents at smoko.

The dust from the road billowed behind him as he drove too fast. Adrenalin spurring him on.

'How lovely, dear,' his mother said as he arrived on the verandah. 'Have a seat and I'll get you a cup.'

His dad grunted and prattled on about the weather. 'Dry out there. Need some rain soon, the ground is cracking. We can't afford another drought…'

Zac let him chatter. His mother returned with a fine china cup and lavished a scone with jam and cream. As he bit into it, Victoria sprang to mind. His mother was a great cook, but these scones were not as light as Victoria's. He shook images of her from his mind.

Stay focused Zac.

With a lull in conversation, he gathered his courage. 'Mum and Dad, I have some news.'

His mother's head popped up. He knew what she wanted. News of finding love; the cocktail party was days away.

'I've signed a contract to purchase the vet clinic from old Chief. He's been talking about retirement for years and is finally doing it. It's mine.'

His mother coughed and snuck a furtive glance at his father.

'Don't be ridiculous boy. We've been over and over this. I'm tired of it when there is so much to discuss about the future of the station.' His father rattled his cup in his saucer.

'It's time to listen, Dad. I will not be running the cattle station. You'll have to find an alternative plan. I'm the new owner of the vet clinic and it's what I want to do. I've been telling you this for a long time.'

His father held his head low and talked through gritted teeth. 'I have one son and four daughters. It's proper process for you to take over the property. And it's tradition. If you do not do this, you are no son of mine.' Jerome stood and left the table.

'He'll come 'round,' his mother said, placing her hand on his.

'He won't, Mum, but thanks for saying so.' Zac noticed she didn't congratulate him on one of the biggest decisions he'd ever made.

Edith rose, patted him on the shoulder like he was a teenager and went after his father.

Usually, he'd race after his father too, reassure him they'd work it out; the future of the family and the station was all that mattered. But it wasn't true. He wasn't going to chase after him and say those words today. Damn it, his father should be chasing after him. But hell would freeze over before that happened.

He was done with these endless arguments. The burden he'd carried on his shoulders for years, loosened, and his body became lighter. This was what he wanted and his family would have to accept it. And even if they didn't, he could do it without their support. He loved his bulldog of a father and his timid mother regardless. At least his sisters would be ecstatic.

Thinking of his sisters gave him a new idea. Why hadn't he considered it before? It was so obvious. Jessica's husband Earl was keen to be involved in the future of beef. The property could stay in the family and the tradition could continue. Ownership might be a little different to what his dad expected but The Coleman Cattle Station could still be in the family.

What a bonzer idea. Zac raced away to talk to his sister.

21

Almost the entire population of the town – at over four thousand people - had turned out for the live *Local Lads Looking for Love* grand finale and cocktail party.

Well, perhaps not the entire town, but the front yard of the *Cedar Creek Plains Farm Stay and B& B* was crammed with people.

The regional television station had found a budget. Fairy lights adorned a white-picket fence leading to a rolling red carpet. It was a bit lumpy here and there from tuffs of under-lying grass. Snow-white balloons were tied to each available post and provided a carnival atmosphere. It looked festive, Tori decided. She also had to agree the event may have copied the idea from the popular mainstream series, but hey, she didn't think anyone would raise an objection about that tonight.

The weather was on their side, with clear, midnight blue skies and a silver crescent moon. The humidity was kept at bay with a gentle breeze and the mood was jubilant with soft background music playing from a live band located over near the sheds mixing in with the pleasant sound of laughter and chat.

Tori inhaled a deep lungful of air. She'd slaved all day on finger foods. Technically she was hired to feed Zac, the contestants and crew. But how could they invite the town and not give them an hors d'oeuvre too? It was inhospitable and un-country like. So she'd made extra, a lot extra.

She set up a drink station on the deck. There wasn't any fancy bar tonight, but she'd roped in a local lad - another one looking for love perhaps - to man the drinking hole.

A hand grabbed her around the leg and Mirry clung tight, her little chest heaving. She was dressed for the occasion in a pink tule dress like one of the fairies who might inhabit the wood; or perhaps she was a princess, who knew? Her daughter fitted in perfectly and could be whatever she wanted to be tonight. Just as quickly as she arrived, Mirry raced away playing chasey with some of the local kids.

There was a stir to her right and she glanced in that direction. Zac arrived to slaps on the back and cheers from the crowd. He wore a dark black suit hugging his shoulders and chest. He matched it with a white collared shirt, the contrast striking. He wore his standard R.M Williams boots and his too-long wavy hair was mussed on top, as always. She curled her fingers in and out, releasing the itch to run them through his head of hair.

The sight of him sent her body into overdrive but she quashed down those feelings. Tonight was his night.

A goose raced across his path, chased quickly by a gaggle of ducks. The menagerie of animals roamed free, never restrained on Nan's farm. Why should tonight be any different? Zac pulled out his phone and captured the retreating animals who scurried amongst the chairs set up on the lawn.

Who would he choose? She couldn't decide. But if he truly

thought he was destined to live a life without children, and he couldn't rob anyone of that right, Clare was the obvious choice. But really? She couldn't imagine it. Clare was so officious and thorough. Tori imagined she needed everything in her life to be perfectly ordered, arranged and scheduled. Not suitable to farm life where things often went wrong.

Clare along with the other girls wouldn't be far away. Tori moved back inside to collect the first platters of hot food. Trays of crackers and dips and cheeses were already scattered around the grounds.

Zac entered the warm kitchen as she removed mini quiches from the oven, her hands in mitts.

He lit up the room. A smile flitted across her face while her skin burned hot and warmth flushed throughout her body. Once again, she ignored the sensations. 'Hey, what are you doing here? You should be out mingling and enjoying your special night.'

'Victoria, I wanted …'

Nan entered, blowing her hair out of her face and puffing out her cream blouse. 'Full crowd out there,' she said and kissed Zac on the cheek. 'Good luck tonight Zac. I hope you find all that you're looking for.' Nan's eyes connected with Tori and her stomach dipped.

Mirry raced through the door, squealing as she exited straight out the back. Mike followed in between the two other children, chasing her with equal excitement.

'Anna is here and needs to see you before we start live streaming.'

Mike had scrubbed up for the occasion but missed the mark with a tux and bright red cummerbund and bow tie.

'Are you the one getting married tonight?' Tori said to him with a smirk.

'Married?' he said. 'Do you know something?' and he turned to face Zac. 'Is this serious mate, you going to propose?'

Zac held up his flat palm. Tori intervened.

'I'm joking. You're dressed like you're the groom at a wedding.'

Mike didn't smile. 'I look alright don't I? Reckon I might have a chance with the rejects?' he asked, his face deadpan.

'No,' Tori and Zac said simultaneously.

Zac's name was being called beyond the door. Tori leaned across, took off one mitt and held his forearm. It was firm under her grip. 'Good luck,' she said. Other words died on her tongue. It felt a little like saying goodbye.

He opened his mouth, closed it again and seemed to be about to say something when the door flew open and in strode Anna Fox.

'Whoa, Anna,' Mike was the first to speak but his eyes were lost on her chest. The low-cut ball gown left nothing to the imagination. It was black, diamantes and gemstones featuring on the fabric, the full skirt billowing around her. Did she get the memo this was regional television?

Tori had purchased a new dress too. It was short, showing off her shapely legs, the long billowing sleeves and frill surrounding the high neck, complimenting her slender figure. Nothing like Anna's but it was light and cool and comfy and she felt feminine in the deep magenta cotton.

Zac still stared at her, his eyes pleading. 'What...' she said but Anna clasped his arm and he walked out of the kitchen backwards and was gone.

22

‘And here we are everyone. We've reached the finale of Zac's search for love!' Anna's voice was loud through the microphone. The crowd cheered.

Zac bounced his knee up and down. He placed his palm on it to stop the shake, then used those same fingers to tug at his too-tight collar. The bright lights made him squint. He'd never wanted to get out of somewhere so much before. He couldn't remember the last time he was so nervous he wanted to vomit.

The three contestants sat on high stools on an elevated timber stage with their legs crossed. He sat to the left and had a clear view of both the crowd and the ladies. Zac didn't want to look at either.

Anna droned on, recapping each of their respective dates and funny anecdotes. Some he'd never heard and he was sure she was making them up for entertainment. Then the questions began. He focused on each one, taking his time to reply.

'What's been your highlight?'

'Are you pleased you came on the show?'

'Is it a difficult choice?'

Anna ran to a commercial break and footage of Zac and the women played on a large screen backdrop. Mixed in were live streams to simultaneous finales around the country region. None of those blokes looked as nervous as him.

And then before he was ready, they were cutting to him. The crowd went silent. He stood and wiped his hands down his pants.

'Clare,' he said and everyone went berserk catcalling and wolf-whistling. 'Shush,' he commanded them with his hands urging them to quieten down. 'Clare,' he began again. 'It was lovely getting to know you. I love your brutal honesty. A man will always know where he stands with you because you'll tell him! You have a no-nonsense approach to life, taking what your heart desires and grasping it, not wasting time on the minor issues. These are all wonderful qualities. We have a lot in common particularly our love of the country and farm life. You must be a fantastic jillaroo and would be a wonderful addition to any team. I think we also have shared goals and common perspectives on life. Turns out your trivia knowledge is not so great.' A light chuckle rose from a small bunch.

He'd vaguely been looking in the general direction of the stage as he spoke, but now he focused on Clare. He shouldn't have. She sat stony-faced and hard to read. Fitted perfectly with the attitude of, her way or no way, that Zac had detected. This woman would break his balls he was certain.

Clare turned her head away and stared at the throng. He followed her direction. Clare stared at Tori standing at the far rear of the group. Zac swung his gaze back. Thinking of her right now would undo him.

'Lucy,' he said next and smiled. 'We enjoyed a romantic date down by the river and a fish. We didn't catch much though.

You're a fun girl to have around and always have a smile on your face and are happy to laugh at yourself. You don't take life too seriously and giggle a lot, it's infectious. I could do with a few pointers. But underneath your pretty face you are tough. And strong. Someone to be admired.'

'Pick her then!' someone heckled from the yard.

Zac paused to settle his nerves. He cracked a smile at her before moving on.

'Sophie. You are the rose and elegance and charm all men seek.' Oohs and aahs drifted up from the audience. Anna chimed in, too.

'He's a catch, ladies, with words like those!'

'Who would have thought a city chick like you could handle the dirt and the dust, and the outdoors as well as you did whilst wearing your designer clothes and immaculate hair styles. But you have. It was a lovely surprise. You are a full package of beauty and adventure all mixed into one. Underneath your exterior is mystery and intrigue that is fascinating but difficult to crack. The man that you let in will be special indeed.' Zac paused. 'But all of you have embraced country life and weren't afraid to pitch in and experience it for all it was worth. You've made this a pleasant experience. Thank you.'

'I …'

'Hold it right there, Zac. Before the big announcement, we're crossing to a commercial break!' Anna worked up the crowd and they cheered and clapped as the ad commenced.

Mike stood with the camera in his face. Tonight he was overshadowed by stationary cameras in strategic locations to capture the stage. Mike wouldn't be cast aside though and was in the way at each opportunity.

'Can I have a drink of water, mate?' he asked Mike who handed one over. Zac drained the glass.

Like a premiership football game when they'd focus with their eye on the prize, Zac zoned everything out. The noise receded and fell away. His heart rate slowed and his muscles relaxed. He was ready.

'The lady I've chosen tonight is someone special. She's hasn't had an easy life but has managed it with grace and humility and achieved great things even though she may not realise it. She's always loved country life, but perhaps forgot how much until recently when that love was rekindled. She is family-oriented, warm, and funny and kind, especially to others and often the first to lend a hand to a person in need. She is fit and works hard and has an opinion on most issues. But by golly, if you scorn her, she'll hit you hard with her caustic tongue.'

People murmured in response, turned to their neighbour, shrugged their shoulders and whispered. The contestants frowned, realising some qualities belonged to them, but not others.

'More than any of that though, she's captured my heart. To be honest she captured my imagination a long time ago and I've never forgotten. I wish I'd taken my opportunity then. But now I'm asking her for a second chance at love. Perhaps she ruined me for others. It was her I pined for in the knowledge of what true love and attraction was. She's had her heart broken and stamped upon, shredded apart and has lost trust. Most men might be difficult to trust, but not me. In me, I will be her greatest advocate. I will help her achieve her dreams. I will stand alongside her, holding her hand and encouraging her. I will protect her heart and nurture it and build her trust until there is no doubt she can rely upon me. I sincerely swear I will never let her down. She has become everything to me, I come alive in her presence, and she makes me a better person. I count the minutes until I see her again.'

'I'm not perfect but I hope she'll accept me as I am. The country vet with a big heart and lots of love to offer. This woman is a great mum and fabulous cook and I hope she'll risk everything again for love. I choose Victoria Christensen.'

Silence descended on the people present. A horse neighed at the fence.

Sweat broke out on Zac's brow. He searched the crowd. Where was she? Isn't this where she finds him and embraces him until he can't breathe and expresses her undying love? She no longer stood at the back. She wasn't inside was she? There's no way he could repeat that soliloquy.

Anna and Mike were muttering. Anna wanted to cross to another show with a real winner, but Mike refused. The viewers would love it or hate it, he said, but either way it was fantastic viewing and he was determined to capture every second.

Clare stood in her satin black pants suit, hands on hips and feet standing width apart.

Sophie brushed her long dark hair off her shoulder and brushed imaginary fluff from her billowing egg-shell blue sleeves.

Lucy, resplendent in a vibrant emerald frock to match her red hair, hung her mouth open and searched the gathered crowd.

Everyone held their breath until the crowd parted and Tori walked towards the stage.

23

Holy shit, Zac Coleman was talking about her.

All of a sudden everything made sense. He made sense. It was like the whole world opened up.

Tears didn't pool in her eyes; bucketloads of water ran down her cheeks as she blubbered. Happy sobbing of course. Tori ripped off her glasses and rubbed at her eyes. She didn't want to lose sight of him. The sea of people standing in front parted leaving a wide path leading her to Zac. Hands shoved her in the back forcing her forward. She both wanted to run to him and simultaneously wait.

The moment he spoke, she'd known. His deep honey voice had caused her stomach to flutter. As his words sank in, her heart hammered in her chest, her eyes pooled with water and she hadn't stopped crying since.

Zac moved one tentative step closer to her and she couldn't control herself any longer. She ran the last few metres to him. Her wedged heels sank into the grass but they reached each other and she collapsed into his open arms. He held her tight. Tori squeezed her eyes shut, blocking out everything else.

Eventually, he let go. Tori wanted to stay safe and secure in those capable and strong arms forever. Zac cupped her head in his hands, peered deep into her eyes and claimed her lips. The kiss was light and gentle. Their third only ever kiss. She sensed him holding back, perhaps conscious of the ogling crowd.

It didn't stop her body reacting though. Heat emanated off him and she melted; they became became one hot wrangling mess together. His stance relaxed as her hands raked down his back and she felt the full force of him, pulling him closer. Her erect nipples brushed against his chest but his lips remained tender. Their mouths met in perfect precision, lip upon lip, wet and warm and inviting. Spirals of ecstasy shivered through her veins and her mouth parted in response. Raising her mouth from his, she gazed at him; he stared back with utter happiness. He pulled back and took shallow breaths. The deep pools of his expressive eyes spoke to her and sent flutters straight to her groin. Her body ached for more of his touch. Thank goodness he showered her with more kisses, to her eyelids and along her jaw and chin until he reached her mouth where he pressed against her with sudden force once more. Every nerve ending tingled.

Something tugged at her chest. A large hand was pinning something to the neckline of her dress and she turned. Bloody Mike. Still being such a pain. Tori moved out of his way but he wouldn't have it.

'It's a mic. You're the winner, the audience wants to hear from you.' He stood back for a minute. 'Who would have thought, hey?' He elbowed Zac in the arm before gaining a better camera position.

The crowd came back into focus as they huddled closer to them, closing the gap. Her cheeks warmed at the scrutiny and she was sure they must be pink. For once, Tori didn't care. The mass responded with hollers and cheers, their excitement palpable and it lifted her. Zac scored a few slaps to the back.

But then Zac was back in her focus.

'No one has ever said such beautiful words about me before,' her voice wobbling yet magnified by the close microphone. Those closest hushed.

'Zac, you are truly the kindest of men. Everyone's best friend. Reliable and friendly and one of the best. I'm so comfortable with you, have always been comfortable with you. I can talk to you and you listen. You are different from other men. You have confidence in me I'm sure I don't deserve and you make me a better person, too,' she hiccupped. Zac tugged a loose strand of her dark hair and placed it behind her right ear.

'You are not a cheater and I'm sorry I ever said that. I know you'd never do that to a woman. You are tender and sincere and true. I don't think you're real.' The crowd laughed. 'Perhaps you are too good to be true,' Tori clasped one of his hands.

'I'm not an easy package. I have a daughter, *an ex-husband,*' she emphasised those words, 'and I'm…with… having another baby. It's a lot for anyone to take on. A ready-made family.'

Zac didn't hesitate to speak up and say what he meant. 'That is exactly what I want and you know why. I might not be able to give us our own children, but your family is my family. We can all be together and I will love your children as I love you.'

Happiness threatened to bubble out of her. Could this all be happening? But for once, the first time ever, she knew without a doubt she could rely on him, trust him.

'It's crazy Zachary Coleman, but I love you too. You've taught me to trust again. I'm prepared to take a second chance and we won't blow it. I believe in you, I trust you, I want you to be by my side forever. I won't let you go, you understand. This is for the long-haul, forever.'

The gathering went from silent to rowdy and back again, captivated as she was with the man in front of her.

'Say something,' she urged him softly.

'You've made me the happiest man alive. I know the future is bright if we can face it together. There's so much to look forward too. And I can't wait.' Into her ear he whispered what he'd like to do to her later. Pulling back, he smiled the broadest she'd ever seen. Then he whooped her up off her feet and she shrieked.

In the background the band commenced playing as Anna Fox tried to call order to the show and Mike fought for footage. There were more shrieks to the right.

'Something just ran over my foot…'

THE END

ABOUT THE AUTHOR

Leanne Lovegrove is a lawyer, wife and mother and a lover of romance and reading. Her law career created an addiction to coffee but provides countless story ideas. The author of four romance novels, this story was her first inclusion in an anthology. Leanne likes writing sweeping love stories with happily-ever-afters with strong female heroines and set in the beautiful landscape of Australia. She lives in Brisbane, Australia with her husband and three children.

If you enjoyed this story, firstly, you should pick up the other four stories that were part of the anthology and Leanne and the other authors would be so grateful if you could leave a review on Amazon or Goodreads. Thank you!

To find out more about Leanne's books, you can find her here:

Web: www.leannelovegroveauthor.com

FaceBook: https://www.facebook.com/leannelovegroveauthor

Instagram: https://www.instagram.com/leannelovegroveauthor/

Bookbub: https://www.bookbub.com/profile/leannelovegrove

HERE'S WHAT REVIEWERS ARE SAYING ABOUT LEANNE'S LATEST RELEASE - A GOOD LIFE:

Lovegrove delivers another standout Australian romance – Duffy the Writer, bookreviewer

This was an amazing ride, amazing story and very creative through-out, very art oriented...loved the setting for the story, I bathed in a rural area of Australia, a little community where everyone helps out with each other, the dynamics and drama with characters I really enjoyed and kept me interested throughout, no way did I wonder at any point away from the story, the plot twists I loved, absolutely enjoyed reading the whole scenario, a bit sad near the ending but this story wouldn't be complete without it as the author weaves this as a well rounded balanced climax to the end. I feel I can't rave about this book enough, I'm overwhelmed by the exquisite talent of this author. Giving this a 5 plus star review/recommendation – Pauline Reid book reviewer

I loved it! Such vivid images of the country side and the characters will stay with me. Great story too – Kate Hunter, Goodreads

Here's what reviewers are saying about Leanne's latest release - A Good Life:

With a picturesque coastal feel as backdrop, A Good Life is a moving story about confronting fears, making amends, and forgiveness. It's about the most simplest of joys and loves, complicated by circumstances, missed opportunities, and the things left unsaid – aplace_inthesun, Instagram, book reviewer

Wow! What a stunning story! A delightful surprise. Once I picked up A Good Life and began reading it, I was hooked! In fact, I had difficulty putting it down until turning the last page. And at that point my heart was bursting with such emotions and love for this story I was speechless. It is a stunning read and perfect on so many levels – Cindy L Spear, book reviewer

Greta Johnson made a dreadful mistake
A Good Life
LEANNE LOVEGROVE

A GOOD LIFE BY LEANNE LOVEGROVE

Greta Johnson *made a dreadful mistake.*

A two million dollar mistake. Unemployed and afraid she flees to her eccentric old aunt, a noted artist living in a ramshackle cottage in secluded rural hinterland. Life has never seemed more difficult.

Brodie Quade *is her aunt's protégé. Born and raised in the region, he paints controversial pieces that depict life's injustices while working at his parent's caravan park. He's going nowhere, but dreams of changing the world.*

Greta represents everything Brodie detests about our greedy and shallow society. Yet in the tranquillity of her aunt's home, they learn to accept each other, and begin to heal old wounds. When all they've gained is threatened by the sudden return of Greta's past, they are forced to face the truth. Has Greta really learned from her mistakes? Is Brodie man enough to do more than confront the wrongs of the world and challenge his own beliefs?

A Good Life is a moving story about forgiveness, acceptance and choosing the right path.

It's available on all online retailers. Get your copy from Amazon in ebook or print here:

mybook.to/AGoodLife

Leanne's other books:

Unexpected Delivery

Illegal Love

Keeper of the Light

Escapades of a Personal Stylist